monsoonbooks

# PARANORMAL SINGAP
# VOLUME 1

Welcome to my world, dear friends.

As I sit in the black corner of the *kopitiam*, looking out into your world, I hunger to invite you to join me.

Do you feel my eyes watching you from the deepest shadows of day, and from the hollow darkness of the ghostly night? Do you sense me sitting on that empty stool beside you, the one that draws your darting eye? And, yes, that flickering sliver of blackness that slides through the half-light among the tables and chairs and sends a shiver down your spine, it is I.

For those who dare, I invite you into my black world. Sit at my table and we'll share a *kopi* and a tale or two.

Then we'll play a little game.

But beware—if you lose, you will be doomed to stay with me in the shadows of the *kopitiam* forever.

Happy reading!

*Andrew Lim*

BOOKS IN THIS SERIES

*Paranormal Singapore*
*Volume 1*

*Paranormal Singapore*
*Volume 2*

# PARANORMAL SINGAPORE

## TALES FROM THE KOPITIAM

## VOLUME 1

Andrew Lim

**monsoon**books

Published in 2008
by Monsoon Books Pte Ltd
52 Telok Blangah Road
#03-05 Telok Blangah House
Singapore 098829
www.monsoonbooks.com.sg

ISBN: 978-981-05-9686-6



Printed in Singapore

12 11 10 09 08 1 2 3 4 5 6 7 8 9

# Contents

# Contents

# Pradeep's garden

'One down, two to go,' Pradeep crooned, knowing full well there were a lot more than two to go. But two sounded better than lots. Pradeep wasn't very good at numbers because they made his head spin, so he didn't worry about them very much.

The branch-lopping shears snipped merrily as he carried on singing his made-up song. The shears were razor sharp.

Years ago his grandfather had taught him how to sharpen the curved blades using a special stone. Now there wasn't a branch on the whole farm that he couldn't snip his way through in an instant.

'One down and 'leventy million to go,' he sang as he moved on to the next one. Pradeep had already cut off three without even realising it. It was so much fun, and no effort at all because the shears could cut through anything. He was proud of just how sharp he could make them. Grandpa would have been proud too but he was asleep. He had been asleep for a long time.

Happily, Pradeep worked on, snip, snip, snipping and chanting as he went. It was so easy. Even his grandfather would have been amazed at just how fast he could go when he wanted to. Snip,

snip, snip went the big shears. It was as if he were snipping off twigs.

Then suddenly Pradeep was at the end of the row. 'Oh!' he said, disappointed that he had finished so quickly. For a moment he was angry with himself for having gone so fast because he liked snipping. He stood there uncertainly under the trees, the long-handled shears hanging loosely in his hands as he wondered what to do next.

'Plant the cuttings, Pradeep!' the voice in his head urged. It was his grandfather's voice.

'Yes,' he replied, 'I'll plant the cuttings. That's what I'll do next.'

Pradeep needed something big to put all the cuttings into. He pondered for a moment. He'd never taken so many before and he needed something really big. Then he remembered the green plastic bucket. It was sitting by the back door. Carefully he placed the shears on the ground next to a basket of freshly picked mangos and a half-empty pitcher of orange juice. It had been full to the brim when he had put it there.

Pradeep went to collect the bucket. He returned shortly and, starting at the beginning of one row, began to pick up the scattered cuttings. There were so many of them. He was careful not to miss any. 'Waste not, want not,' came his grandmother's sharp voice. For a moment Pradeep stopped and looked around, then he smiled. Grandma was asleep in the house just like Grandpa,

Mummy and Daddy. The voice was in his head.

When he had finished picking up the cuttings, Pradeep stood still for a moment and listened to the noises all around him. Birds were squabbling and singing in the trees, and he could hear the distant sound of the traffic on the road. It was so peaceful, so quiet. There was no sound from the nasty, noisy children at the school nearby.

Pradeep looked down at the bucket. It was filled almost to the brim. He smiled happily. It would be a big crop.

'You'd better be good when you grow up or I'll cut you off again,' he said loudly, looking down at his cuttings. He picked one up and examined it closely. 'You'll grow up nice for Pradeep, won't you?' he said as he turned it in his hand. It was delicate and pink with a deep red tip at one end. Pradeep nodded and dropped the cutting back into the bucket. 'Grow into a nice friend for Pradeep,' he said softly as he turned towards the garden.

The teacher and her class had come to the garden that morning after Pradeep had gone to the school. He'd invited them to come and pick mangos. Pradeep had given them the orange juice with the special stuff in it. It was the same stuff he'd put in Grandpa's tea when he'd scolded him: the powder Grandpa used to put the birds and rats to sleep.

The children now lying under the trees used to yell at Pradeep as well. Now everyone who had yelled and not been nice to him was asleep. The pretty teacher had been kind. She hadn't yelled at him, but she had drunk some of the orange juice so now she was asleep as well.

Lifting his heavy bucket with both hands, Pradeep started towards the garden behind the house. He would put the fingers in the ground, and soon they would grow more boys and girls, but these boys and girls would be nice boys and girls who would become his friends. And the nice teacher, she would be there. He would like her for his grown-up friend. Whistling happily, Pradeep opened the gate and walked into the garden where Grandpa used to help his little plants grow into big ones.

There, sticking out from the rich soil, were Grandpa's fingers, all ten of them because Pradeep knew that thumbs were really fingers too. And next to Grandpa's fingers were Grandma's, then Mummy's and Daddy's, and the lady next door and . . .

# Head of the class

'Children, pay attention, please,' Miss Margaret Stephenson, teacher and spinster, tapped her ruler on the edge of her desk. On the blackboard behind her she had written several verses of poetry and today's lesson was about to start.

Miss Stephenson had been a teacher for most of her seventy years. First it had been in her homeland where she had taught at a girls-only school in Somerset for fifteen years. Then she'd answered an advertisement in *The Daily Telegraph* for an English teacher to join the staff of a very distinguished girls-only school in Singapore.

Miss Stephenson had had absolutely no problem in acquiring the position. She had no dependants. Both her parents were dead, she was an only child and, of course, there was no man in her life—or ever would be. Miss Stephenson didn't like men very much, and the thought that one might someday actually attempt to press his attentions on her rendered her almost to the point of hysterics. No—no man would ever sully her virtue.

When she'd first arrived, Singapore had been very much to Miss Stephenson's liking. Despite the sticky heat, she'd adapted quickly and enjoyed the rather relaxed pace. Yes, men had paid her attention, many men, and some had seemed quite eager to spend time in her company. However Miss Stephenson had made it clear that she was not interested.

For thirty years she had taught the girls of Singapore. She hadn't just taught English but also manners and deportment. She'd also always encouraged high moral standards in all her students.

Eventually, when she was sixty-five years old, the school had asked Miss Stephenson to retire. They'd decided that she was a little out of touch with the new generation of young ladies and her behaviour was becoming a little erratic.

There had been a number of incidences.

Miss Stephenson had naturally objected to both their judgement and to her enforced retirement, but she had had no choice but to accept it.

The first few days of her enforced retirement had been long and quite frustrating. Then one day, quite out of the blue, she had come up with a solution: she would establish her own small private school for young ladies.

Luckily Miss Stephenson had earned a good salary from her teaching position, and with her material needs being few she had managed to save a large amount of money. She had also been left a considerable sum through her parents' estate—money she had invested wisely.

She'd sold her small apartment in Bishan and purchased a house in Pasir Ris. The house had used almost all of her available funds, but she was pleased. There was room for her, room for a dormitory that could accommodate twelve young ladies and room for a large classroom.

'Miss Stephenson's Private Boarding School for Christian Ladies' soon opened for business.

Unfortunately things got off to a very slow start. The very thought that she had to advertise her new establishment had passed Miss Stephenson by, and at the end of the first term she'd had absolutely no students whatsoever.

The first day of the second term, she'd stood at the front of her classroom and gazed at the twelve empty desks, as she had done every morning of the previous term. No smiling faces had beamed back at her but she was used to that.

Throughout her career there had been few smiling faces in her classroom, but she had long since forgotten that. In fact, Miss Stephenson had been rather a severe teacher, and the faces that had stared back at her had often been close to tears and full of extreme trepidation.

There and then she'd promised herself that soon all her children would smile adoringly back at her.

Later that day, as she'd read *The Straits Times*, she'd seen something that had made her smile. It had been the answer to her prayers. Soon, she thought, she would have pupils in abundance.

Now in year three, Miss Stephenson's Private Boarding School for Christian Ladies had twelve attentive students at their desks, just as they had been since the day Miss Stephenson had dreamt up her brilliant idea.

'Now, children, I want you to recite after me the words of William Shakespeare from *King Henry VIII*.' She turned towards the blackboard and pointed her ruler to the words written there. 'And, when I am forgotten, as I shall be, And sleep in dull cold marble . . .' Her voice droned on as she recited the words but there was no other sound. Not one single voice joined her. Nonetheless Miss Stephenson read on, and when she'd finished she turned to her class and beamed. She laid down her ruler and clapped her hands.

'Well done, class, well done. That was lovely. As a reward you can all go outside and play for an hour. Go now!'

Miss Stephenson clapped her hands again, but the faces at the desks didn't move. She didn't seem to notice, and instead walked out of the classroom and went to the kitchen to make herself a cup of tea.

'They are lovely girls, and they are having fun,' she said, hearing the voices of excited children in her head as she stood at the window staring out into the tiny, deserted back yard.

With a cup of tea in her hands, Miss Stephenson walked through the dining room, its long table set with thirteen place settings, and carried on into the dormitory. She gazed lovingly at the twelve beds, each one containing a sleeping child—a sleeping headless child.

Miss Stephenson turned and went back into the classroom. There, propped on each desk, sat the head of a young girl. Eyes stared blankly to the front of the classroom.

At night, when it was time for the girls to sleep, she would gather the heads and tenderly carry them to the dormitory to reunite them with their bodies. In the morning, before she woke the girls for breakfast, she would return the heads to the classroom, ready for the day's lessons.

Miss Stephenson sat at her desk and drank her tea, oblivious to the heads and their blank stares.

The children are playing in the garden, she thought. Later, they will have their dinner, go to the bathroom then bed and tomorrow, bright and early, they will say their prayers, have breakfast and class will begin again.

Up until that point, the police investigators had not solved the island mystery that was now almost three years old: the mystery surrounding the theft of twelve embalmed bodies. It had been in all the papers. Students from an exclusive girls-only school had died when their bus veered off Benjamin Sheares Bridge. When the police retrieved the bodies, they'd acted quickly to embalm them to give parents, many of whom lived overseas, enough time to fly to Singapore.

However, one night the bodies had been stolen from the morgue and never seen again.

Miss Stephenson finished her tea and went back to the kitchen. She rinsed her cup, put it on the counter then paused, staring at the big freezer that sat in the corner of the room.

'I must do something about them,' she muttered, walking to the freezer door and opening it. Inside were two men. She thought that perhaps they were from Java. They had been the men who Miss Stephenson had hired to steal the bodies from the morgue. They'd delivered the girls, disposed of the van then come back for the rest of the money she'd owed them. Miss Stephenson, however, had not been about to waste any more money on them—she had a school to run. She had made the men lime juice laced with rat poison. At first it had been difficult for her to stuff them into the freezer, but she had managed in the end.

'Now, girls, time for supper. Wash up and come to the table,' Miss Stephenson called as she let the freezer lid fall shut. Sometimes, just sometimes, she realised exactly what she was doing but fortunately, she concluded, those moments were becoming fewer and fewer, and that suited her admirably. Soon she would have those moments no more.

'Quickly, girls, supper is getting cold.'

# Little boy bad

We moved into our apartment on a Saturday. There were just three of us but we didn't realise that there was already someone else living there.

My name is Lim Poh Choo. I am a widow. My husband died in a fire aboard the ship he worked on as an engineer. I have two children, Su Lin and Ming Xiang. Not long ago we shifted to a smaller apartment in an HDB estate in Bedok because we could no longer afford to live in the bigger one we had in Tampines.

The children were excited by the move, as children often are. Our new apartment had four bedrooms. It wasn't too old and I thought we'd been lucky to get it, especially for such a low rent.

When we first moved in, I wondered about the fourth bedroom. It was a dull room and strangely cold, despite the fact that the walls were painted white and there was a window. However, the paint on the ceiling seemed darker. I thought that perhaps white paint had been thinly painted over a darker colour.

'Just a bad paint job,' I'd concluded. I decided that, because the other bedrooms were larger and brighter, this could be used as storage for the moment. I had plenty of other things to do, so I moved all our boxes and surplus furniture in there. I decided I'd sort it out when we were properly settled.

The first week we were very busy. The new school term was about to start and I had to go to my job as an administrator at East Shore Hospital. At least by shifting closer, my travel time from the new apartment was shorter. That meant I could be home when the children returned from school. So life got into a normal routine and I forgot the sorry state of the extra room.

The second week everything was fine. The children settled in and started their new school. I met several of our neighbours. They were friendly enough, but I felt that perhaps they wanted to tell me something. They didn't, but there was definitely something unsaid that, in hindsight, should have been.

It was three Saturdays after we had moved in when the first incident took place. It was raining outside. Ming Xiang had gone to play football with his new school friends and Su Lin was playing inside while I worked in the kitchen, tidying shelves and finally putting everything in its place. Su Lin was in the fourth bedroom. She had taken to using it as her play space, and that was fine. By then I'd folded flat the cardboard boxes that we'd transported most of our goods in from the other apartment. I was going to have them taken away when the opportunity arose.

Because Su Lin was so quiet, I went to check on her. I found she had popped some of the boxes back into shape and was using them as the walls of her make-believe house. She had used some of the flattened boxes to make a roof and was having guests for dinner. Her dolls sat around her plastic tea set. She gave me a big smile and asked if I wanted tea. I told her that I would have a cup later.

To one side of the house of cardboard was an old cabinet. It had belonged to my late husband's mother. He'd liked it while I hated it. Why I had brought it to the new apartment, I didn't know. I had decided that when the boxes went, that would go as well. I left Su Lin and went back to the kitchen. She closed the door for more privacy, I think.

Later as I was having an iced tea, standing watching the rain, I heard Su Lin's voice. She sounded upset and angry.

'Stop that!' she was scolding. 'You stop that!' I thought that she was just acting, as children do, but she sounded close to tears so I quickly went and opened the door.

Su Lin was sitting in her box house but the sheets of folded cardboard that had made up the roof were lying to one side. Her plastic tea set and dolls were lying all over the floor.

'He pulled the roof off my house,' Su Lin wailed through her tears.

'Who did?' I asked indignantly.

'The bad boy did!'

'I don't see a boy.'

'He's sitting right there!' Su Lin said pointing.

I looked to where Su Lin was pointing, directly at the old cabinet. At first I thought that perhaps one of the other children from another unit had somehow slipped in to play with her and was hiding behind the cabinet.

I went and had a look behind it but there was no one there. I thought that perhaps it was just an imaginary playmate. I played along and in a very stern voice I told the bad boy to play nicely. I put the roof back on Su Lin's house and left the room, leaving the door ajar.

I made another iced tea. Ming Xiang would be home soon and, as with any eleven-year-old boy who'd been playing football in the rain, I knew he would be muddy and in need of a shower.

Suddenly there was huge crash and Su Lin screamed. I ran into the bedroom. The roof of her playhouse was off again but worse, the big cabinet was lying face down on the floor. It had crushed the side of Su Lin's box house and almost landed on her.

'Mummy, it was him. He pushed it over!' She was pointing to the spot where the cabinet had previously stood. There was nothing there but I felt the hairs on the back of my neck stand up. Just then Ming Xiang arrived home.

'Come and see your brother,' I told Su Lin and, helping her out from amongst the boxes, I hustled her out of the room. Ming Xiang was wet but not that muddy, so I made him rub himself down and change his clothes. Ming Xiang is good with his six-year-old sister and they both settled down in the fourth bedroom to play.

About an hour after Ming Xiang had arrived back at the

apartment there was another big crash from the room. I ran to see what had happened. The door was closed so I opened it, not knowing what to expect. Rushing inside I saw that the cabinet had fallen over and almost crushed Su Lin. It had gouged a big hole in the wall.

'He's a bad boy,' Su Lin cried, running towards me. Ming Xiang was standing by my side. 'Bad boy,' she repeated, wagging a finger at something or someone only she could see. 'He's not nice at all.'

Ming Xiang looked at me and pulled a face that told me he thought his young sister had gone completely mad. At that point I didn't even consider that it could be a spirit. I didn't know what had happened. Despite being Chinese, my mother had taught us that ghosts and spirits were all nonsense, and I suppose I grew up believing that. So right then it simply never crossed my mind that there could be some supernatural force at work. I was an educated woman, and educated people didn't believe in ghosts, did they?

I decided to leave the room exactly as it was and closed the door. The rest of the afternoon the children played with their PlayStation in the living room while I made dinner. Everything was fine until I went to the bathroom later that evening and passed the fourth bedroom. The door was open. I closed it, but when I came back from the bathroom it was open again.

'Did either of you open the door?' I asked when I went back

into the living room. Both the children were now engrossed in the TV and told me they hadn't even moved. I wondered if the lock was faulty. I shut the door again, then waited a moment to see if anything happened. It stayed shut. I went to the living room and watched TV with the children before we all went to bed.

That night was the first of many terrible nights. First it was Ming Xiang. He woke up yelling. I rushed into his room.

'Someone was pulling my hair and punching me,' he said, more angry and confused than scared. I gave him a cuddle and he eventually settled down. It was then that Su Lin appeared in the doorway to Ming Xiang's room.

'The bad boy came and jumped on my bed,' she said. 'He's not nice, Mummy. Tell him to go away.'

'Go away, Bad Boy,' I said sternly, shaking my fist. I wasn't feeling brave and my heart was pounding. Something very strange was going on. There was a bang. The door to the fourth bedroom had slammed shut.

'Sleep in my bed,' I told the children. Fortunately it was the double bed that my husband and I had shared, so there was room for us all. I didn't sleep well. I awoke many times, imagining I could see shadows moving across the room.

In the morning I went to the bathroom, then went to check on Su Lin's room. It looked as if a tornado had hit it. Bedclothes, clothes and toys were everywhere. Ming Xiang's room was the same. It hadn't been a mess when I'd taken the children to my own bed the night before.

'What's happening?' I whispered, and almost as soon as I'd said it I felt an icy breeze blow on the back of my neck. I rushed into my bedroom and shut the door.

Later that afternoon I was tidying up while the children were out playing with their new friends. At one stage I noticed that the door to the extra room was open again. I found one of my late husband's screwdrivers and did what he used to do—I wedged it under the door. Now nothing could open it, not from the inside at least.

That evening we all went to the hawker centre by the beach and had a nice meal. It was good to get out of the apartment. When our taxi dropped us back home, we took the lift to our floor and opened the door. I gasped. Our apartment was an absolute mess. At first I thought we'd been burgled or that a freak wind had somehow blown the windows out and messed everything up. Cushions, ornaments, CDs, DVDs, books and pictures were scattered everywhere.

I started to cry and so did the children.

The bedrooms were no better. The door to the fourth bedroom was open and the screwdriver I'd wedged under the door was now embedded in the wall beside the door. The big cabinet was lying on its side. The cardboard boxes were everywhere and the other pieces of furniture were either upside down or lying haphazardly around the room.

'The bad boy did it,' Su Lin was saying. 'Bad, bad, bad boy. Go away!'

I was so angry. I couldn't see this 'bad boy' she spoke of, but for the first time I had to admit that something terrible and not at all natural was going on. Suddenly I realised why the rent for this apartment was so low. They knew! Everyone knew that something bad was happening here. The neighbours had been about to tell me but for some reason they hadn't.

I cleaned up the children's rooms and put them to bed. Then I started cleaning everything else up. It was midnight before I'd finished, and I had to go to work the next day. Eventually I managed to get to bed, but no sooner had I gone to sleep than the children were climbing into bed with me. Su Lin's bad boy had pulled their hair and thrown things around their rooms.

'Go away,' Su Lin yelled at one stage as she hid behind a pillow, staring at a shadow in the corner of my bedroom.

It was then that something happened that convinced me there was definitely a spirit in the apartment. My bedroom door opened then slammed closed. For me that was it. I grabbed the children and we all went into the living room. I placed two mattresses on the floor and when the children had fallen asleep, I made tea and wondered just what I was going to do. I waited until morning then telephoned the hospital, telling them I had an MC and wouldn't be coming in. I hated the lie but we had a sick apartment that needed curing.

When I came back from dropping the children at school, I went next door to my neighbour, Mrs Wong. She'd been the first neighbour to greet us when we'd arrived. She was just about to invite me into her apartment when she stopped.

'You've seen him.'

'Bad Boy?'

'Bad Boy, yes,' she replied.

'My daughter sees him. I just see what he does.'

'Come in,' Mrs Wong offered. 'I'll tell you the story. I wanted to tell you when you first came but I thought you would think I was interfering. It was better that you met him yourself. Then you would believe me. The last three tenants lived there only a few days each. You have been the longest since it happened.'

As we sat down over a hot drink, Mrs Wong began to tell me the story.

The people who had lived there a while ago had been drinkers. There was a husband and wife, and the husband's brother. The husband and wife had two children, while the husband's brother had one child. His wife had left him. According to rumours she'd gone back to Malaysia. The brothers had many friends and sometimes parties that went on late into the night. The police were sometimes called.

One night there'd been a quarrel between the two brothers. Both had been yelling and Mrs Wong's husband had called the police. However, before they'd been able to get to the house a fire had started in one of the bedrooms. The police later said that they suspected some of the children had been smoking, but they would never know for sure. Both the brothers had been too drunk to even notice the fire until it had been too late; by then the apartment had been full of smoke.

The children had all managed to escape except for a little boy.

The police and firemen had turned up as soon as they could and the brothers had been dragged off. But no one had been able to find the brother's wife. They later found out that she'd spent the night at the house of a friend.

No one had realised that one of the children had been trapped inside.

When the firemen had managed to put out the blaze, they found the body of a little boy in the back bedroom. The smoke had killed him. The apartment was uninhabitable for many weeks after that while it was repaired.

'Then new people started to come,' Mrs Wong continued, 'but they didn't stay long. Everyone talked about the bad boy but only the little ones could see him—and now you. You are the first to come to me.'

'What can we do?' I asked, not expecting Mrs Wong to have

the answer, but she did.

'No one asked me before,' she replied, 'so I didn't want to look like a busybody.' Then she proceeded to tell me her plan.

It was so very, very simple.

I'd been baptised a Catholic when I was a child, but when I married my husband, a Buddhist, I stopped practicing Catholicism. After he died I would sometimes attend mass at church.

So I took my courage in my hands and phoned my priest. I explained my problem and before lunch, Father Tan was at my door.

The good Father explained about how to lay a spirit to rest. Because the young boy had died such a lonely and horrible death, he hadn't found his way to the spirit world. Instead he remained in the place he'd died, lost, scared, angry and frustrated.

Father Tan had incense, holy water and his bible. He asked me to wave the incense while he walked through the apartment, sprinkling the holy water and reciting a special prayer. It took perhaps ten minutes, then we both said a prayer together and it was over. Father Tan stayed for a cup of tea then left.

The first thing I did was walk into the bedroom where the young boy had died. I was shocked. It was no longer grey and cold. The furniture and the big cabinet stood just where I'd left them. The boxes were all flattened and neatly stacked. The sun was coming through the window. Even the black shadow on the ceiling seemed to have dulled. It was over! The little boy's spirit had moved on.

Now we are all at peace and it is a lovely feeling.

# Sandman's corpse

Siloso Beach was a popular picnic spot for the Abdullah family. With five young children between the ages of four and eleven, and only one average income, there was not a lot of spare cash to go around. They certainly couldn't afford grand outings and expensive treats. However, the cost of packing some snacks, taking the MRT from Hougang to HarbourFront, then taking the free bus to Sentosa suited them perfectly. This had become their Sunday family outing.

When they got to the beach, Abdullah, the head of the household, would sit and read the papers while his wife, Fauziah, would lay out the food on a blanket under the shade of a palm tree. The children would always race straight to the water's edge. As the beach was always crowded at the weekends, the Abdullah family arrived early to claim the best spot with the most shade from the scorching sun.

One Sunday last year they went to Siloso Beach as usual. It was a bit overcast so there weren't that many people around, something the family were grateful for. They also weren't worried about rain as they'd come kitted out with umbrellas. Keeping a watchful eye on the children as they splashed around the water's edge, Fauziah laid out their snacks. There was *mee goreng*, *kari ayam* and *kerupuk* for the kids, and *nasi lemak* for her and Abdullah. It was her husband's favourite. She'd also brought him *air bandung*, also his favourite.

After lunch Fauziah and Abdullah sat side by side under their palm tree. While her husband read the newspaper, Fauziah watched the children. Theirs was a companionable silence, apart from Abdullah's occasional grunts of disgust when he read an article he didn't agree with. The children had run back to the water's edge and were building sandcastles.

Fauziah turned her attention to another group of children who were also playing further along the beach, just in front of a big artificial rock. They were scooping sand from the water's edge using buckets, laughing and shouting as they did so. Then they would carry their buckets to a spot behind the rock where they seemed to be using the sand to build something. Because of the rock, Fauziah couldn't see exactly what it was they were building, but they were certainly enjoying doing it. She smiled, happy they were having fun.

A while later the tide began to turn, and the Abdullah family all knew that soon the sandcastles they'd been lovingly building would be washed away. The oldest child, Rosman, bounded towards them.

'You must come and see what we have made,' he urged. This was a ritual.

'When Ayah's finished reading the paper,' Fauziah replied, as she always did.

'Okay. We'll build a wall to stop the sea until you get here.' Rosman bounded back down to where his siblings were waiting. It was then that Fauziah noticed that the other group of children further up the beach had gone. She could see their parents packing up to leave and only a handful of people still remained. The grey sky and threatening clouds signalled a monsoon shower was on its way.

'We'll go and look at their sandcastles,' Abdullah suddenly announced, putting down his paper and placing a shoe on top to stop it blowing away. They got up and walked towards their children. They didn't need to hold hands; theirs was a good marriage and they were comfortable together.

The sea was fast dissolving the hastily built sand wall, but Fauziah and Abdullah arrived just in time to see the results of their children's hard work. They'd built a large fort and surrounded it with a moat. A bridge had been constructed across the moat and smaller forts were scattered all around. No doubt the two eldest children, Rosman and Rosnah, had been responsible for the main elaborate fort while the younger children had made the simpler structures. But despite the division of responsibilities, Abdullah and his wife judged their children equally, showering all of them with glowing praise, as parents do.

As the wall finally collapsed and the sea rolled in, Abdullah and Fauziah turned to walk back up the beach. It was time to leave. The rain was coming. But Fauziah hesitated.

'I want to see what the other children built,' she said. 'You know, those kids that were further up the beach.' Abdullah sighed but fell in step with his wife. The artificial rock was not far away.

When they rounded the rock, they came across a very accomplished sand sculpture. It was of a life-size man. The children had dressed him in a suit, pressing wet sand to create the shape of lapels, buttons and a breast pocket. They had even given him a collar and tie. His face looked European, and he was wearing a pair of glasses made of sand. His arms were at his side, and there was a sand briefcase in his left hand.

'Wow!' Abdullah exclaimed. 'Very good, very good indeed.'

'Yes it is,' Fauziah agreed. 'A pity the sea will wash it away.' The first licks of the tide were reaching the sand briefcase just as the first drops of rain began to fall.

'We must hurry,' Abdullah said, setting off for their palm tree. Fauziah hurried after him, calling for the children.

Suddenly the rain began to fall in earnest, and the Abdullah family were the last to leave the beach—well, almost!

The advancing tide was washing over the sand briefcase—except it wasn't made of sand but real leather. A wave washed over the hand that was holding the briefcase and washed away a light covering of sand, exposing human fingers. On one of the fingers was a large gold ring with a diamond set in it. The next wave revealed a gold Rolex watch on the man's newly exposed wrist.

And so the sandman lay in the shadow of the artificial rock, each wave turning him into a very real corpse. Eventually the storm became so strong it washed the body out to sea.

When investment banker Denis Cromwell, who'd been visiting Singapore from the United Kingdom, didn't return to his suite at the Rasa Sentosa Resort that same Sunday evening, his company was informed. They, in turn, called the Singapore police and Cromwell's steps were retraced.

It was revealed that the previous evening he had attended a business meeting at the Sentosa Resort and Spa and left there on foot, saying he would walk back to his hotel and wanted to stretch his legs. He was never seen again.

Foul play was considered. After all, Denis Cromwell had been a wealthy man and the founder and CEO of the highly successful investment bank Cromwell and Sparks. But no ransom demand was ever made.

A week after his disappearance his decomposed body was discovered, tangled in fishing nets off Sentosa. According to the coroner, he'd died of a heart attack.

The Abdullah family, oblivious to who the sandman really was, still visits Siloso Beach every Sunday. They're easy to recognise. Just look for five children and a picnic blanket laid out under a palm tree. Abdullah will be sipping his *air bandung* and reading the paper while Fauziah will be watching the children. They will appear to be a picture of absolute contentment.

But how different their lives would have been if the tide had come in just a little bit faster that Sunday afternoon last year.

# The wisdom tooth

'I'm sorry, it will have to come out.'

'But I've never even had a filling.'

'Perhaps, but this is an impacted wisdom tooth and if it doesn't come out you will remain in the most terrible pain.'

'Okay,' Adrian Lee agreed after a long pause. 'Okay, you're the dentist.'

'Yes, I am,' the man behind the white mask replied. 'You'll have to trust me.'

'When will you do it?'

'Tomorrow afternoon at 3 pm,' the dentist replied, lowering his mask. 'That time is free isn't it, Nurse?'

'Yes, Dr Nair, it's free. One hour?'

'Yes, one hour,' the dentist agreed. 'Mr Lee, please arrange for someone to come to the surgery at 4 pm to collect you. I will use a general anaesthetic. Have you ever had a general before?'

'No, never.'

'Have any of your family members ever had a bad reaction to anaesthetic?'

'I don't think so. I'll check with my mother.'

'Okay. We will see you tomorrow.'

Adrian rapidly escaped from the dentist's surgery on Orchard Road. His girlfriend, Amy, was waiting for him at their favourite coffee shop in Takashimaya.

'Tomorrow I get butchered,' he said morosely as he sipped his latte. 'Tomorrow a piece of me will be gone.'

'Stop overreacting,' Amy snapped. 'It's only a tooth and you've done nothing but spend the past month complaining about how much pain you're in.'

'But what if . . .? What if . . .?' Adrian stuttered.

'But what if what?'

'Why do they call it a wisdom tooth?' he queried. 'What if when they take the tooth out I lose all my wisdom?' Amy snorted into her coffee.

'Don't be so silly! A wisdom tooth is just called a wisdom tooth; it has nothing to do with anything. I've had two out and did I suddenly become a dummy?' She glowered at her boyfriend before adding: 'Don't answer that. It'll be fine, Adrian. I'll take the afternoon off work and come and pick you up. I'll take you home, put you to bed and it will all be over, okay?'

'Okay.'

'Okay.'

'You'll just feel a little drowsy.'

'Okay, Doctor,' Adrian replied. He was past caring. The sedative now running through his bloodstream had relaxed him so much he felt no anxiety towards anything. If the dentist had produced a chain saw and suddenly announced he was going to cut his head off, he would have just grinned and told him to get on with it.

People pay a lot of money to feel this good, he mused a fraction of a second before his world went black.

There was a light. Adrian was slowly waking up.

'Here he is,' he heard Dr Nair say. 'He'll be disorientated for some time, but once he's had a few hours sleep he'll be fine. Give him one of these as soon as you get him to bed but not before.' He held out a plastic bag containing some large pills. 'There will probably be some bleeding so put a towel on his pillow, and if the bleeding hasn't ceased by the time he wakes up, apply this gauze with cotton wool and make him bite down on it.' The dentist dropped a gauze and a small packet of cotton wool into the plastic bag. 'Keep it in place as long as he can and that should allow the wound to clot. If that fails, call my emergency number and we may need to add more stitches. If he has any discomfort, Panadol is recommended.'

'Right, Doctor,' Amy took the plastic bag from the dentist. Dr Nair, the nurse and herself managed to get Adrian from the recovery couch to a wheelchair. The nurse then led them to the exit while the dentist went off to tend to his next patient.

During the taxi ride to Stevens Drive, Adrian drifted in and out of sleep. When they reached his parent's condo, the taxi driver helped Amy carry the patient inside. Both of Adrian's parents were at work and Amy was grateful for the extra pair of hands. When they'd managed to get Adrian into bed, Amy gave the driver a tip for his troubles. Alone with her decidedly out-of-it boyfriend, Amy stripped him to his underwear and managed to get him under the bedclothes. With the dentist's instructions clear in her mind, she got a towel to cover the pillow and held Adrian's head up so he could swallow the sleeping pill. Then, positioning him on his side in a semi-recovery position, she quietly shut the bedroom door and went to the living room to watch television until Adrian's mother got home from work.

'He's sleeping,' Amy told Mrs Lee when she arrived home that evening, 'as sound as a baby. The dentist said there were no complications at all.' She recited Dr Nair's instructions regarding bleeding, then accompanied Adrian's mother into the bedroom for a moment.

The patient was lying on his back, his face pale against his black hair. There was a small amount of dried blood at the corner of his mouth. For a moment both women thought he might be dead, then he stirred and rolled slightly onto his side. They breathed a sigh of relief.

'They say it's the anaesthetic that is the dangerous thing in any operation,' Mrs Lee said as the pair exited the bedroom, quietly closing the door behind them.

'I've heard that too,' Amy agreed. 'I'd better be getting along. My boss gave me the afternoon off but I have to put in two hours tonight to make up the time.'

'You're such a good girl. Thank you so much for looking after Adrian. I'll call you when he wakes up.'

'Thank you.'

It was dark when Adrian opened his eyes.

'Argh uh,' he grunted. 'Argh uh,' he repeated again and again until the bedroom door opened and the light was switched on.

'Adrian, are you awake?'

'Argh uh, argh uh, argh uh.'

'Adrian, what is it?' Mrs Lee was becoming alarmed. Her son was staring at her but his gaze was completely blank.

'Argh uh, argh uh, argh uh,' he repeated over and over again.

'Adrian, what is wrong?'

'Argh uh, ARGH UH!'

'Adrian?' Mrs Lee was almost screaming. 'Adrian?'

'ARGH UH!' he yelled, his eyes wide and empty.

Adrian Lee was no longer home.

# Chicken feed

The day started out well enough. Yeo Ah Teck was alive, and being alive at ninety-two was always a good way to start the day, at least Ah Teck thought so.

Despite his age he still lived alone but his eldest son, Stephen, and his daughter-in-law, Eunice, lived next door. The Yeos owned a chicken farm in Lim Chu Kang and both houses sat side by side at the front of the small property. Behind the houses were three chicken sheds, and in each shed there were 5,000 chickens.

The hens were not in cages but roamed freely around the large sheds. The wire netting on each side of the shed allowed a breeze to blow through. The hens laid their eggs either in nest boxes raised above the floor or on the sawdust floor itself. The sawdust and droppings were cleaned out weekly and sold as fertiliser.

The Yeos were proud of the fact that their chickens were not locked in cages with their beaks clipped. It was because of this they had, years before, adopted a phrase their youngest son Richard had seen in America: Free Barn Raised.

Yeo's Free Barn Raised Eggs were popular with many leading Singapore restaurants and the small business prospered quietly, much to the satisfaction of its owners. It was an idyllic lifestyle.

It was a typical Sunday. Stephen and Eunice had gone to church as usual. Afterwards they would visit friends then return home for dinner with Ah Teck in the evening. It was still early and Ah Teck was alone on the farm. The six staff, who would gather the eggs and pack them every morning and evening, had the day off. They would go back to the farm later that evening.

On Sundays it was Ah Teck's task to feed the hens. It was an easy job. In each of the chicken sheds there was a large feed hopper in the roof. All he had to do was go to the hopper and pull the rope. That would open a valve and the grain would run down chutes into the feeding troughs. But this particular morning things did not quite go to plan. As Ah Teck made his way through the hungry, noisy hens, something quite unexpected happened. He had a stroke.

Ah Teck knew it was a stroke. He'd suffered a minor one many years previously, but this one felt much more serious. He couldn't move a muscle, not even one. He couldn't even blink and that was a problem, considering that he was lying on his back, flat on the floor of the first shed, surrounded by 5,000 hungry hens.

The problem with hens, as Ah Teck well knew, was that despite the fact that they didn't have teeth, they did have beaks—sharp beaks. As he lay staring up at the shed's tin roof, his eyes locked wide open, he felt exceptionally vulnerable.

It didn't take long before the first hens came to inspect him. One or two tentatively pecked at his bare legs; as usual he was wearing baggy old shorts. Some pecked at his bare arms; as usual he was wearing an old tattered singlet that exposed his skinny old arms.

Surprisingly the pecking didn't hurt. The birds were just examining him, perhaps trying to force him to get up and release their feed. After a few minutes a pair of hens climbed onto Ah Teck's head. Another stood on his bony chest, peering down at his face. It suddenly pecked him right between the eyes. Then another hen stood on his shoulder and pecked at his cheek.

Oh dear, Ah Teck thought, not quite recognising the severity of the situation. At ninety-two he had grown accustomed to life's little ups and downs. Had he been able to he would have laughed at just how ridiculous the whole situation was. Most people said that it was his sense of humour that had kept him alive for so long.

Now more hens had gathered around him and he could feel their beaks on his exposed legs. They were still pecking. Others were clambering over his head and the frequency of their pecking was increasing, along with the force. He was sure that the din in the shed was much louder than before.

Then the first beak struck his left eye and the pain made Ah Teck want to scream but his vocal chords were frozen in his throat. Then his right eye was struck, then again and again and again. Soon Ah Teck was blind, but that didn't deter the hens. Instead they began to claw at his bare skin.

Oh please, God, the paralysed man pleaded silently. They were tearing at his ears and his lips, and he could taste the blood that ran into his open mouth. Please, God, take me, he pleaded as the hens massed over him, fighting each other for the tasty treat that had suddenly appeared in shed number one.

'I wonder where Pa is?' Eunice asked as she and Stephen pulled up in front of their house. It was dusk but there were no lights on in Ah Teck's house.

'Perhaps he's with the workers,' Stephen replied. He noticed several bicycles propped up against the fence.

The first scream of many suddenly rang through the night.

One of the workers, a young girl called Xiao-ling, had found what remained of Yeo Ah Teck. The double tragedy was that Xiao-ling's life would never be the same again. Never again would she sleep in peace—and never again would she eat chicken curry.

# The poker player

The freighter *Armedes*, a Greek-owned Singapore-registered vessel, was sitting amongst a score of others, anchored off Sentosa Island, waiting to enter the harbour and dock to unload its cargo.

It was a stormy night. The sea was choppy and rain lashed the vessel. It was a night for watching television or, as most of the crew members were doing, playing cards.

It was a tradition for the crew to play card games the night before they docked at their home port. Many of the sailors would go ashore poor, while a lucky few would go home with bulging wallets.

This night the game was poker, straight stud, take no prisoners. No 'cash up and leave', this was winner takes all. There were six chairs and as one player fell out, another would take his place. With a crew of thirty-five, there was no shortage of players. Most of us there were from Singapore or Malaysia, and gambling was our favourite pastime.

The table was surrounded by spectators. The game had already been going on for quite some time. We had been stuck off the mainland for almost two days already, mainly because of the bad weather that had prevented many vessels from docking. The game had started the previous evening. The rule was that players could leave the table only to go on their scheduled watches. When their watch was over, they rejoined the game. That was the way we did it aboard the *Armedes*.

I was a spectator. I never play. There was a lot of money on the table, and already five of the players had dropped out. Others filled their chairs. The reason I never play is because not only am I bad at cards, but I never seem to have any luck at anything, so I prefer to keep my wages safely in my wallet until I can go to the bank.

It was almost midnight. I was bored of watching the game and decided to go to my cabin. As second cook aboard the ship, it was my job to prepare breakfast the following morning. It didn't matter if we were moving or at anchor, the routine never changed for us, card game or not.

I had just stood up to leave when the mess door burst open. There was a very tall man standing in the doorway. He was dressed in a long black coat that skimmed the deck's surface. He was wearing a broad-brimmed hat and a pair of dark glasses. His face was ashen and I wondered for a moment if perhaps he was ill. However, from the way he forcefully stepped inside the room and shut the door behind him, I knew that he was fit and well.

'Can I play?' he asked in a deep voice.

'When there is an empty seat,' replied Big Lee, the bosun and unofficial keeper of the game. Big Lee never played. His job was to watch and make sure no one cheated. He was a referee of sorts. In return the eventual winner would give him ten per cent of the winnings. The bosun was a big man—which explains why he was called Big Lee—but he also had a particularly nasty temper and hard fists.

No one ever argued with him.

'Very well,' the stranger said. 'My name is Mr Ng.'

'And your first name?' Big Lee asked.

'Just Mr Ng,' the stranger replied.

'How did you get aboard?' Big Lee wanted to know.

'I swam,' the stranger replied, then laughed loudly. Everyone else laughed too, thinking his explanation preposterous, and the mood relaxed.

'Boatman must be crazy to come out in this.' The bosun played along with Mr Ng's idea, certain he was just joking around.

At that moment Azahari, the kitchen boy, threw his cards on the table and stood up. He offered Mr Ng his seat at the table.

'I'm finished,' he said. 'The chair is yours.'

'Thank you,' Mr Ng replied as he glided around the end of the table and slid into the chair.

'Would you like to take off your hat and coat? I'm sure you'd be more comfortable,' Big Lee asked.

'No thank you,' replied the stranger. 'I won't be here long.'

He chuckled. 'Not long at all.'

'I will take all your money,' said one of the seamen.

'We shall see,' replied the stranger.

It was then that I noticed that Mr Ng had almost no nose and very big, thick lips. I imagined that without his big black glasses on he would've been a most unusual-looking person. He was starting to fascinate me so I decided to stay. Mr Ng reached into the pocket of his shiny leather coat and removed a thick packet of banknotes. Big Lee took the money and handed it to Mr Sim, our banker. I also noticed then that Mr Ng was wearing gloves, very fine gloves. I had never seen a card player wearing gloves before.

Mr Sim was our mess man. He was old, far too old some would say to still be working, but he said he had nothing else to do and the *Armedes* was his home. His wife had died many years ago and he had no living family, so he was permanently on board.

As far as we knew Mr Sim had no first name—or if he had, we didn't know it. Calling him Mr Sim was, in a way, a tribute, an honourable thing for an honourable man. He was honest and had been the banker at our card games ever since I'd joined the crew some five years previously.

Mr Sim sat on a chair to one side of the card table and beside him, on another smaller table, sat a box of money and a box of chips. Mr Sim quickly counted the stranger's money then counted out stacks of chips. There were many. He passed them, one stack at a time, to Big Lee who pushed them across the table to the stranger's elbow.

Then the game began—and what a game it was. Mr Ng turned out to be a spectacular poker player. He bet big and while he didn't win every hand, he won many. Soon the stack of chips by his elbow had grown larger and larger. Players left and others took their places. When all the players had lost their money, the game would be over.

At one point Mr Ng pushed a large stack of chips towards Big Lee and asked him to change them into cash. Big Lee passed them to Mr Sim and soon there were stacks of banknotes beside Mr Ng as well as chips.

Again and again Mr Ng won, hand after hand. He began changing his chips into cash more and more regularly, and after a while he started stuffing the notes into his coat pocket instead of leaving them on the table.

Some of the other players became disgruntled as they lost round after round to Mr Ng. The stranger was winning far too easily and far too often. After a while only Mr Ng and three others remained at the table. Those who did remain had few chips left—apart from Mr Ng, of course. I glanced at Big Lee. He looked worried, staring intensely at the stranger to see if he was cheating.

Personally I don't think Mr Ng was cheating. I think that not only was he a wonderful card player, but he had an uncanny streak of luck on his side. He changed more chips for cash and it was obvious that soon the game would be over. I couldn't help but think that Mr Ng was readying himself for a rapid departure. Perhaps his boatman was due back to pick him up.

It was 4.30 am. I realised that there was little point in me going to bed. I would have to be up at 5.30 am to prepare breakfast. So instead of bed I made some tea and returned to the game.

The last few chips were in the middle of the table and Mr Ng soon won them. That was it. The game was over. Mr Ng collected all the chips and pushed them towards Big Lee.

'I think the game is over,' Mr Ng said in his deep voice. 'It is time I was going.'

'Hm,' Big Lee grunted, passing the chips to Mr Sim. It really didn't matter to Big Lee who won the game because he knew he would get his ten per cent. But as Mr Sim counted out the cash, it became clear that the stranger had no intention of giving Big Lee a cent. When the money was passed back, the stranger took it and stood up.

'I collect ten per cent of the winnings for running the game,' Big Lee stated.

'Really?' Mr Ng replied. 'Then you will have to follow me outside to collect it.'

With that Mr Ng thrust the remaining money into his coat pocket and glided towards the door. Big Lee lunged after him, shouting angrily. Several of the other players joined in.

But before they could reach him the door opened and Mr Ng was gone. Big Lee and half a dozen others ran after him, yelling at him to come back. I started to follow them but suddenly I saw something that stopped me dead. Under the chair where the stranger had been sitting was a pool of water. A wet trail, as wide as a mop would make, ran from the chair to the door. Something was sparkling in the wetness, like little pieces of glass or shiny confetti. I squatted to take a closer look and dabbed my finger in the water. One of the sparkling things stuck to my finger. It was silver and blue. It was a scale, a fish scale the size of my fingernail.

Just as I was standing upright Big Lee stormed back into the mess followed by the others. They were all dripping wet from the driving rain.

'Did you catch him?' I asked.

'No,' Big Lee replied bitterly. 'He must have gone over the side of the boat. He must have drowned. The water's like a washing machine out there. All that money, all *my* money, gone.'

I didn't say anything else. There was no point.

I often think about that night and the mysterious Mr Ng who appeared from nowhere and disappeared overboard. Very strange!

I have never told anyone about the scales I found. That was years ago. The crew still talk about Mr Ng, especially when there is a game of cards aboard the *Armedes*. I wonder if he'll ever show up for another game.

# Promise from the other side

My husband died many years ago. I never remarried. Instead, I dedicated myself to looking after my two daughters. I was a seamstress then, some say a good one, and I promised myself I would bring up my two adorable daughters the best way I knew how. It wasn't easy and all too often money was tight, but we managed.

My youngest daughter, Meng Meng, married a European called Robert Spears who worked at the British High Commission. It was a good marriage and after a few years they moved to Australia with his next posting. Felicia, my eldest daughter, continued to live with me, sharing our home.

Felicia was a wonderful, warm, giving girl. She was very pretty, very outgoing and had many friends. She never married; instead, she dedicated herself to her career, working as a senior accountant in a bank. She looked after me as I got older and we were happy together, although I was sad that she never married.

'I haven't found a man I want to marry, Ma,' she told me whenever I brought up the subject. She dated some nice men but while they were interested, she simply wasn't.

Two years ago fate dealt our family two terrible blows. They say things happen for a reason, but none of us ever found out what that reason was. The first terrible incident was that Meng Meng's husband was killed in a car accident in Sydney. Suddenly Meng Meng was alone thousands of miles away with their two children, Sophia and Brian. They were then aged seven and eleven respectively.

There was insurance money but not a lot. They had already bought a house in Sydney and there was a heavy mortgage to pay. At that time the housing market was very depressed so, rather than stay and wait for things to get better so she could sell the property for a higher price, Meng Meng sold the house at a loss. She wanted to return to Singapore to be near her own family. Felicia took leave from the bank and flew to Sydney for the funeral. She stayed on to help Meng Meng organise her affairs and sell the house. Then she came home, bringing Meng Meng and the children with her. The apartment that Felicia and I shared became very, very crowded, but we were family and we needed to be with each other, especially at that sad time.

The second devastating blow came just a few weeks after Felicia had arrived back in Singapore. She was diagnosed with cancer. It was already too late to treat. It was terminal. Felicia had always been an organiser and she did just that. When she knew that she was dying, she sat us down and told us what was happening. There were many tears but through it all she told us we needed to move to a bigger apartment. She said that even when she was gone the family would need more space. So the decision to move was made, despite the fact that we didn't have much money.

We managed to sell the apartment in Bishan for a decent price. We added that to Felicia's savings and Meng Meng's insurance money and were able to afford a much larger apartment in Yew Tee, but money was still very tight.

'Ma, don't you worry about money,' Felicia said to me one night just after we'd moved into the new apartment. 'I will make sure that you have enough money, I promise.'

After a while Felicia became too ill to work. We all knew that she would be dead within a few weeks, but she was still worrying about her family. Before we'd moved out of the apartment in Bishan, Meng Meng's container of furniture and possessions arrived by ship from Sydney. To make room for us all in the small apartment we took a lot of our furniture, including some beautiful cabinets Felicia had collected over the years, and stored everything in a rental warehouse until we could move into our new apartment.

When we first moved into the apartment in Yew Tee, we only took the furniture that we needed at the time. The place would need painting first. It was an old apartment and we had a lot to do before we fully moved everything in. We didn't know then that, what with Meng Meng's furniture from Australia plus ours, our new apartment would be too crowded and we would have to sell what we couldn't use.

Inevitably poor Felicia died. She died at home, nursed by us to the very end. We were all devastated. Her friends gathered along with the family, and the funeral was a large affair. The bank was very generous and paid for the funeral because they held her in such high esteem.

After Felicia had been cremated we tried to get on with our lives. However, money was always an issue. My eyes and fingers were failing and I could no longer work as a seamstress. Meng Meng, who didn't have formal job training because she'd married and had children at a young age, got a job in a fashion store at City Plaza. It didn't pay much.

Meng Meng and I decided it was time to sell off the furniture we had in storage. A lot of it was Felicia's, and while I wasn't happy to be selling her treasures, I remembered her promise to me: 'I'll make sure you have enough money.' I knew that some of her furniture was worth quite a lot of money so perhaps that was what she'd meant.

Meng Meng and I decided that we would each chose one of Felicia's pieces to keep and sell everything else. I chose a beautiful old Chinese rosewood cabinet and Meng Meng an old oak writing desk with a roll top. It was very English. The rest we sold, including the remainder of Meng Meng's furniture from Sydney and some furniture of mine. The warehouse was cleared out and that meant we didn't have to pay for storage any longer.

About eleven months had passed since Meng Meng, Felicia and the children had come back from Australia. That was when the first part of Felicia's promise came true. It happened, as these things do, in a very strange way.

Felicia's rosewood cabinet that I had decided to keep was in my bedroom. I hadn't used it, but one day I suddenly felt compelled to sort out the papers inside and perhaps reline the drawers so I could store some of my clothing there. I went to the cabinet and started work.

One of the drawers had papers in it. These were not legal papers; Felicia had made sure that they'd all be neatly organised in a folder in the cabinet beside her bed. The papers in the drawer were programmes from shows she had been to and travel brochures for the trip around Europe she would never go on. It made me very sad. There were moments of fun captured in ticket stubs and programmes from the concerts, shows and movies she'd seen. There were birthday cards from family and friends, lots of photographs that I couldn't bring myself to look at and there, at the back, was a travel agent's folder from her sad journey to Sydney.

I don't know what made me open the folder. Well, yes I do—Felicia made me open it. Inside the folder were her travel itinerary, customs information and extra baggage labels that she hadn't used. Also there, hiding between some of the papers, was a lottery ticket. The ticket had Golden Casket written on it. It was an Australian ticket. I picked it up and was just about to put it back in the folder when I remembered Felicia's words to me.

I decided to ask Meng Meng what she thought, but when she came home from work that evening she was tired, frustrated and had sore feet from standing all day in the shop. It wasn't the right time to tell her about the ticket. Later, after we'd had dinner and she'd relaxed, I told her about the ticket and the feeling I had that Felicia had guided me to it. I thought for a moment that my daughter was going to laugh at me but, as she told me later, at that moment she could hear her sister's voice saying that she would look after us.

'But how can we check it?' I wanted to know. 'The lottery is in Australia and we are here in Singapore.'

'Don't worry, Ma,' Meng Meng replied. She went to the computer she'd brought back from Sydney and set up in one corner of the living room. She tapped away at the keyboard then asked me where the ticket was. I had left it in the kitchen. I went and collected it and gave it to her.

'I have gone to the Golden Casket website, Ma,' she said. 'All the winning numbers are kept there.' She checked the date on the ticket then clicked away on the keyboard for a few moments. Suddenly she stopped. Her eyes darted from the computer screen to the ticket then back again.

'Oh,' she said after what felt like an eternity. 'Let me check again,' she said and a few more seconds went by. Then Meng Meng turned to me. 'Ma, we have won AUS$350,000.'

'Oh,' I replied. I had to sit down. It was such a lot of money. 'Thank you, Felicia,' I whispered. 'Thank you, dear daughter.'

The prize money had to be collected within a year of the date on the ticket so we had only a few weeks left before it expired. Meng Meng gave up her job and flew back to Sydney two days later. She was back in Singapore a week later and a money transfer for the lottery win was in our bank account. We were no longer poor, thanks to Felicia.

So there it is. From beyond the grave my lovely Felicia has been looking after her family, making sure that we have the money we need to live well. We are blessed, and every day I thank my beautiful daughter.

# The devil's blade

I love to collect unusual things. My apartment is crammed full of them. My friends and family say I am like a magpie, a bird renowned for collecting shiny objects and hiding them in its nest. Perhaps I am like a magpie, but that's just the way I am.

This is my story. The story of how I found *it*.

One day I was in Mr Tan's antique shop in Chinatown. I used to go there often when I felt like collecting something special. I have been there many times over the years, but it was only on this particular visit that I noticed it, hidden away on a shelf in a dark corner at the back of the shop.

It was a dagger, about thirty centimetres long. At first I wasn't sure if it was made from bronze or brass because it seemed to be tarnished, almost black. The blade was thick in the middle with blunt sides. One end, the point, was quite sharp—sharp enough to open a letter or cause someone a serious injury. It was surprisingly heavy but the thing that attracted me the most was the handle, or rather the end of the handle.

Picking it up to examine it more closely, I accidentally rubbed the end that had been covered in a rather sticky black substance. As the substance smudged, I could see a glint of something. Holding the dagger towards the dim light above, I suddenly got quite a shock. Whereas the blade was battered, rusty and bore signs of heavy use—or misuse—the end, by contrast, was quite ornate. It appeared to have been carved by hand and not cast. I realised that the glint I had seen earlier was a tiny piece of red glass, possibly a ruby, set in the dagger's handle. As my eyes adjusted to the light, I suddenly saw what the carving was of and almost dropped the knife in fear. Under the tar-like substance was the shape of a goat's head, complete with curling horns.

In hindsight I should have put the dagger down immediately and walked out of the shop. I didn't. I don't know why but I felt I had to have it. Walking back to the front of the shop, I started to rub the tar from the handle. Mr Tan, who had been serving another customer, saw what I was doing.

'Don't do that,' he yelled. 'Don't touch it unless you buy.'

'But I want to see if it has another eye,' I told him.

'Yes, yes, yes,' he replied, agitated. 'But don't clean here.'

'But I want to be sure.'

'Then you take home. Bring it back if there is no other eye and I'll give you your money back.'

In all the years I had been visiting Mr Tan's shop I'd never seen him so upset, and we've had our fair share of hard bargains. This time, as always, I haggled with him but, for some reason, I sensed that his heart wasn't really in it. He let me have the dagger for only $35; I'd been prepared to pay at least twice that. Whether or not it was my imagination, I thought I saw my old adversary heave a big sigh of relief when I left his shop carrying my new treasure.

As I sat on the MRT on the way back to my apartment in Sengkang, I could feel the weight of the dagger on my lap, wrapped in newspaper and stuffed in a plastic bag. It felt heavier than before. When I alighted, I went to my sister's apartment. I would always show her the latest treasure I'd bought, but not this time. She didn't approve of knives and suchlike, so during my visit I kept the package hidden under my chair.

Only when I was safely in my apartment did I unwrap the dagger. I took a cleaning solution and a cloth from the kitchen and began to wash the dagger, removing all the tar and grime from years of neglect. That was when I realised that it was indeed bronze and yes, I had another stone, a green one, to go with the red one I'd already spotted. Both sat together like eyes, staring menacingly up at me.

'Aiyoh,' I thought as I polished the dagger. When I had finished I admired my new find, turning the goat's head on the handle this way and that. From some angles it looked like a benign old goat, but from other angles it looked like a drawing I'd seen in a book—a drawing of a devil's mask. Cannot be, I thought to myself. Part of me wanted to put the knife in the back of a drawer and forget about it, while another part of me wanted to put it on display. It was fascinating, ugly and beautiful all at the same time. The goat's head and its expression changed depending on the light; one moment it was benign, the next just plain evil. Did I really want to display it?

Eventually I decided I had to. I put it with some ornaments in a glass cabinet next to the door. That way anyone coming in or leaving my apartment would see my new acquisition, not that I have many visitors these days. The older I get, the fewer people want to see me.

That night my dreams started. Normally I don't dream, or if I do, I don't remember them. The dreams I do remember, however, are dreams of another time, when I was younger. Dreams of when my wife, May, was alive. Dreams of the times before my son William went to sea, never to return, and before my daughter Andrea was stillborn.

But the dream I had that night was still with me the following morning. It was more of a nightmare than a dream. As I ate my breakfast I recalled that there had been flickering fires, and naked men and women daubed with blood. They'd danced in the dirt, circling a stone slab that was raised above the ground. Light from dozens of torches filled the air. I shuddered as I remembered a man, wearing a mask like a goat's head, striding amongst the dancers. He'd been very tall and, like the others, his body had been covered in red paint or clay that looked like blood. He'd had a long tail that he'd carried behind him. It had curled and twisted like a serpent.

Under his arm I remembered that he'd been carrying a young European girl. She'd been blonde, very pale, no more than nine or ten years old. She'd been screaming in terror, but the man in the mask had shown her no mercy. He'd thrown the girl onto the stone slab and effortlessly held her there, one hand around her throat as her flailing limbs had struggled to be free.

Suddenly I dropped my forkful of *chee cheong fan* as I remembered that he'd been holding a dagger above her—my dagger! I recalled how the red and green eyes had flashed in the flickering light. The dancers had surrounded the altar, chanting like baying hounds for the scent of blood.

I remembered I'd woken in a sweat just as the dagger had plunged into the girl's heart. Even then, as I sat in the tranquillity of my kitchen, my heart was racing. I needed my inhaler. I took it from the kitchen drawer and breathed in deeply. Eventually my heartbeat slowed. I made some tea to help me relax.

As I sat in the kitchen finishing my breakfast, I looked over at the dagger. It was still where I had placed it in the cabinet by the door. In the cold light of morning, the eyes were no longer sparkling. I went and picked it up. The dagger felt heavier than before and the green and red stones looked dull and faded. No matter which way I turned the handle to the light, the stones refused to sparkle. Puzzled, I put it back in the cabinet and went back to finishing my breakfast.

Only when I went to take another mouthful of *chee cheong fan* did I notice the stain on my hands—a dark, red stain. My hands were covered in blood. I dropped my fork, hearing it crash to the floor. My eyes darted to the dagger. It, too, was covered in blood. My heart began to pound again, but it wasn't just my heart—someone was also pounding on the door.

'Mr Seah, Mr Seah, there's been a murder!' It was my neighbour, Madam Chua. Like me she lives alone. She sounded terrified. I quickly took the dagger and washed the blood off it, then pushed it to the back of the cabinet before washing my own hands and drying them on my dressing gown. I went to the door and opened it to find Madam Chua pale-faced and very distressed.

'Madam Lim on the third floor, she's dead, stabbed last night. The police are here. Oh, Mr Seah, what is happening?'

With that Madam Chua collapsed at my feet. I managed to carry her to my sofa and poured her some tea.

Soon the police knocked on my door and asked me lots of questions. After a few hours, Madam Chua went back to her apartment. Shortly afterwards I saw her drive off in a taxi. Another neighbour told me she was going to stay with her sister in Bukit Batok.

It was only later that day that I reflected on what had

happened. With dread I looked again at the dagger. The stones were still dull. There and then, without having any answers to the questions the police had asked or the many I was asking myself, I knew the dagger would have to go. Whether or not it had had anything to do with Madam Lim's death or my nightmare, it was evil. I wrapped it in newspaper and left the apartment with it tucked under my arm.

I usually walk a lot because that is what keeps me healthy at my age. From my many walks around Sengkang I knew that there was an old drain tucked away on a grassy area where a pig farm used to be. The drain was covered with a metal mesh grate and hadn't been used for many, many years.

The place was deserted when I unwrapped the dagger. The eyes on the handle were sparkling, one red, one green. The goat's face looked evil. I quickly pushed the dagger through the mesh covering and let go. After a short time I heard it hit the bottom. The dagger was gone. I was free of it once and for all.

That night I allowed myself a shot of whisky and went to bed early. I was tired, very tired. Nightmares had robbed me of peace the whole day. I couldn't help thinking that perhaps they'd also robbed Madam Lim of her life. I am not a man who usually believes in demons and superstition, but as I lay in bed trying to sleep I felt uneasy. Eventually I nodded off.

The nightmare came again: flaming torches, dancing figures

and the same giant red creature with the sweeping tail and the mask shaped like a goat's head. The girl was there again, as was the knife and the blood.

I awoke as before, my heart pounding in my chest. I sucked on my inhaler and waited for the palpitations to cease. As I was lying there I noticed the blood. It was dried blood and smeared across both of my hands. For a moment I thought that maybe I'd banged my hand in the night and skinned it on the bedside table, but I had no cut or bruise on my forearm. Then I had a terrible thought.

I leapt out of bed and hurried to the door. There, in the glass cabinet, sat the dagger. Once again there was no spark in the gemstone eyes and, once again, the blade had blood on it.

What to do? I washed the dagger and found newspaper and a plastic bag. I decided I would take it back to Mr Tan's shop in the morning and give it back to him. I wouldn't ask for money. I just wanted it to go away, go back to where it had come from.

It was still early, around 3 am, so I decided to make some tea. It was only when I was boiling some water that I heard voices and a scream from below. I froze. A few moments later police sirens filled the pre-dawn silence. The whole apartment block was ablaze with lights. There had been another murder.

The headline in *The Straits Times* the following day was: SECOND

MURDER IN SENGKANG HDB. Sitting on the MRT on my way to Chinatown, I managed to read the article over the shoulder of the passenger next to me. My dreadful package was in a plastic bag on my knees.

I didn't know the second woman who'd been murdered. She'd been quite young, a mother of two. Her husband, it seemed, worked the night shift. She'd been alone in the apartment when she'd been stabbed. The children were unharmed. Her husband had raised the alarm when he'd returned home in the early hours of the morning.

I alighted at Chinatown station and made my way to Mr Tan's shop, which was off Banda Street. Turning the corner I suddenly saw that the shop was closed. There was no sign of life and a sign with the words 'For Sale' hung in the window.

Confused, I stopped dead, uncertain what to do next. My stomach lurched.

'He's gone to his son's place in Hong Kong,' a man yelled from across the street. He ran a stall selling knick-knacks to tourists and I remembered him from my last visit. 'Mr Tan said that one day you might come to find him and to give you this.' The young man approached me and handed me a small envelope. My name had been hand-written on the front. I thanked him and he left.

I put my dreaded package at my feet and tore the envelope open. There was a single sheet of paper inside.

*Dear Mr Seah,*

*If are reading this, it means that you have discovered the curse of the dagger and I am so very sorry for you. I lived with that curse for many years, although I fortunately learned how to make it lie still.*

*How I came by the dagger is not important but once I had it, like you, no doubt, I tried to make it go away.*

*When I realised it was evil I threw it in the river, but the same night it was back with me—back where it always sat on the shelf at the rear of my shop.*

*But there is a way you can be rid of it.*

*When I first came into its possession, the man I bought it from wrote me a letter like this one. He said that the only way to stop the nightmares and the terrible things happening was to cover the eyes on the handle with tar so that it could not see. For when it has made a kill and is satisfied, only then the eyes will close.*

*If you cover the eyes and blind it, it will lie still.*

*But beware, for when the eyes are uncovered the dagger, having been starved for years or perhaps centuries, will return with a terrible vengeance.*

*The letter I was given warned me that I could not give the dagger away. It was to be mine until someone else bought it from me. Only then would I be free of the curse. Someone else had to bargain for the dagger and money had to exchange hands.*

*The letter also warned me that to tell anyone of the curse, or force someone to buy the dagger, would make it and the curse mine forever.*

*So whoever buys the dagger from you cannot be warned.*

*I am so sorry.*

*I wish you luck with beating this terrible curse.*

*Mr Tan*

*PS: My neighbour has the key to the shop. You may use it until the dagger is sold.*

*There is a pot of tar in my room at the back. Cover the eyes of this accursed thing and prepare to bargain for your life.*

And that is how, at my age, I became a shopkeeper, or rather, the proprietor of an antiques shop. Business is surprisingly good, although the one object I need to sell the most has attracted no buyers. It sits, as it must, at the rear of the shop, its head covered in tar.

I have stripped my apartment of almost every ornament I have spent years collecting. Every one of my treasures is in my new shop. I live in the back, using it as a traditional shophouse was once used. My apartment sits empty although my neighbours pretend that I am still there. For appearances sake I stay there some nights, but for the most part I am here.

I can see a young couple, tourists, at the door. They are coming in and I must go to greet them.

'Hello, I am Mr Seah. Welcome to my humble shop.' The couple are handsome, or rather he is handsome and she is pretty. They return my greeting in heavy American accents. We make small talk as I gently steer them towards the back of the shop. Perhaps today will be the day. I can only hope.

It has been almost six months now. There have been no more stabbings at the apartments, and the murderer of the two women has never been found.

'What is this?'

The man has seen the dagger and picked it up. My heart skips several beats.

'It is an ancient bronze dagger,' I tell him, 'very old indeed.'

'Okay,' the man replies, weighing the dagger in his hands. He holds it up to the light to examine it more closely. 'What's this stuff?' he asks, rubbing away the tar with his forefinger.

'We think it is tar,' I reply, 'put there to protect the carving of the head.' I feel a twinge of panic. Will he uncover the eyes? I keep talking. 'The dagger was cast but an artist later carved the head on the handle.'

'Okay,' the man says. His wife wanders off, looking at other objects more to her taste. For a moment the man hesitates. I think he will put the dagger down and follow her, but no. He frowns and stands there, weighing it in his hand, tracing the outline of the carving through the tar with his fingers.

'A solvent will easily remove the tar,' I say, desperate for him to make me an offer.

'How much?' he asks and my heart begins to pound. I have to bargain with him. I have to make it realistic or the curse will remain mine and mine alone.

'Eighty Singapore dollars,' I reply.

'Thirty,' he snaps back.

'Seventy.'

'Forty dollars, final offer.'

'Forty-five,' I plead. 'It cost me almost that.'

'Done!' The American smiles and reaches for his wallet.

With shaking hands I give him change for his fifty-dollar note. I take the cursed dagger to the counter and wrap it in newspaper. Then I place it in a plastic bag and hand it to him.

'Thank you,' the man says. He flashes me a self-satisfied grin. 'I collect old bronze. This looks very valuable.' He delivers his final statement with a smug look on his face.

I can see that he is already thinking about what he will tell his friends. How he made the deal of a lifetime with an old Chinese man in Singapore. How he duped me.

He steps out into the sunlight. The woman is waiting. I know I should make some effort to get his address so I can send him a letter too, but his arrogance makes me bite my tongue.

As they walk down Banda Street I can hear him tell the woman how clever he is. They both turn and grin back at me. I wave and they are gone.

I turn back to the shop. The 'For Sale' sign is sitting behind the door. I put it in the window and telephone for a removal truck. Now I can go home.

# Ghost at my door

I hadn't seen my friend Farouk for almost two years. I had been working in KL and he had been based in Hong Kong but flying between Hong Kong, Tokyo and Manila.

We both worked in IT but Farouk was the real whizz kid. His company shuffled him around, sending him to wherever things needed sorting out. I knew I wasn't quite in the same league as he was, but I was well paid for what I was doing. Part of me was a little jealous of his glamorous lifestyle but Farouk reassured me that living in a hotel wasn't as great as it sounded.

Farouk and I had been best friends since school, and we'd stayed in touch. Both of us had blog sites and we'd SMS each other all the time about girls, the latest gadgets and football, which we were both nuts about. So although we didn't meet in person that much, we were still close. Just as it always is with true friends, you stay on the same page and when you do get together, even if you haven't seen each other for years, it's like you have never been apart.

So that's why, when I changed jobs and moved back to Singapore to live with my parents, I was surprised one day to answer the door and find Farouk standing there with a big grin on his face. What surprised me the most was that I'd just spoken to him that morning by SMS. He'd been in Hong Kong and told me that he was due to fly out to Tokyo that very morning for at least a fortnight. Coincidentally my father, who is a lecturer at NUS, was also in Tokyo that week attending a seminar.

When I saw Farouk standing there on my doorstep, however, it didn't register with me that he was actually supposed to be on his way to Tokyo. I was just pleased to see him and I figured he'd simply changed his plans and come home to surprise his family and, yes, me.

I invited Farouk inside and my mother, who had always liked him and regarded him as a son, offered to prepare lunch. Even though Farouk had an apartment in Hong Kong, he was no cook and frequently ate out.

'I really came here for some of your mother's home cooking,' he whispered to me when she'd gone into the kitchen. It was Saturday and I'd been watching an S.League match on TV. We sat and watched the game, chatting while Mother cooked for us—or rather, cooked for Farouk. She reheated some beef *rendang* and *sambal udang*. It was a great meal and Farouk told Mother so.

When I asked him about his trip back to Tokyo, he just shrugged.

'Some things are more important,' he replied offhandedly, which surprised me. 'Seeing you and sampling some home cooking was worth it, but I must be going soon.'

Shortly afterwards, Farouk gave Mother a kiss on the hand, as is Malay custom. I walked him down to the void deck, thinking he would then catch a cab, but he told me he wanted a walk. He gave me a hug.

'I'll be seeing you, Shamsul,' he said softly, then walked away. He stopped at the corner of the block to wave, then he was gone.

Back in the apartment, Mother and I talked about Farouk's surprise visit. It was now late afternoon and as I settled down to watch TV, my programme was interrupted by an urgent news bulletin. A sombre-faced reported was at a crash site, behind him was the charred skeleton of an airplane. The reporter was saying that an aircraft, en route from Hong Kong to Tokyo, had attempted to land at Narita International Airport in a terrible storm and burst into flames upon impact with the runway. There were no reported survivors.

As the reporter was talking, images of a broken, smouldering aircraft flashed across the screen. I knew right at that moment that Farouk had been on that flight.

I just knew it.

An hour later, while Mother and I sat glued to Channel News Asia for updates, Farouk's sobbing father telephoned with the news that Farouk had been on that fateful flight. My mother and I said nothing to his parents about the visit—and still haven't. For them to know that Farouk came to see me and not them would break their hearts.

My mother and I now share a bond that is even more special. We don't talk of Farouk's visit—we don't need to. Even if we did tell my father, or anyone else for that matter, they would probably think we were mad.

Perhaps we are.

# Sanctuary tree

It grows beside the temple wall. The Buddhist temple itself is ancient. No one knows its history because the records were lost years ago. Bodhi trees surround it in abundance, but there is one tree that stands out above the rest. Known as 'the mother tree', it is almost nine metres wide and about thirty metres tall. Many believe that a Bodhi tree can hear your prayers and bring peace and prosperity, which is why they are so respected.

This is the story of the Sanctuary Tree of Simpang Bedok.

'The temple is no longer functioning. I have ownership of the land. The temple will be pulled down along with the trees.'

'This is not good, Mr Cho. This is not good at all. This is a special place. It should be left in peace.' The speaker was a man named Ghazaly, a foreman for the developer's company.

'You are Muslim,' Mr Cho responded sarcastically, 'what do you care about an abandoned Buddhist temple?'

'It is a place of worship,' Ghazaly replied stubbornly. 'It doesn't matter what my faith is, Mr Cho, this is a place of worship. You can leave it and build around it.'

'Don't be silly,' the developer snapped. 'Pull those trees down now. If you haven't made a start by tonight, I'm letting you go.'

As Mr Cho angrily turned away, a stranger suddenly appeared. She was old and dressed in black. She stood between Mr Cho and his Mercedes. In her hands she held two sticks for support. She planted one on each side of her, effectively barring the developer's way.

'Please move so I can get into my car,' Mr Cho ordered. He was irritated by his foreman's disobedience and this old crone was blocking his way.

'Not before I tell you a story,' the old woman replied. 'You must hear the story of the Sanctuary Tree.'

'Don't be ridiculous!' Mr Cho snapped. 'Why should I listen to a silly story? I am a businessman. My time is money. I have things to do so step aside.'

'You must listen to the story. You can't cut down the tree or destroy the temple. It will be your downfall.'

'I don't believe in your mad superstitions. The trees are coming down and so is the temple.' Mr Cho signalled to his driver and the man revved up the engine. The developer smirked at the old lady and stepped around her, slipping into the back seat of his Mercedes.

'You will be cursed,' the old woman shouted. 'You silly, greedy man, you will be cursed.' Mr Cho ignored her and told his driver to take him home. The old lady slumped against her sticks and almost fell over. Ghazaly rushed to catch her.

The foreman gently led the old woman to a large piece of masonry that had fallen from the temple wall. It was all he could find by way of a seat. Then he fetched a water bottle and gave the old lady a drink. He was quite anxious because the frail old woman looked quite pale. She was very dark-skinned, but her wrinkled face was grey with fatigue.

'Have you travelled far to be here?' Ghazaly asked. The old lady met his eyes and nodded.

'Yes, I have travelled very far to be here today. I knew that something bad was about to take place here.'

'What is this Sanctuary Tree you speak of?'

'This beautiful tree is the Sanctuary Tree,' she replied, pointing to the giant Bodhi that towered above them.

'And what is its story?'

The old lady took another sip of water, straightened and breathed in deeply. Suddenly the colour flooded back into her face and her dull eyes became alive.

'Yes,' she said softly, 'if I tell you the tale of the Sanctuary Tree, then you can tell that man and he will see why it cannot be cut down.'

'I'll try,' Ghazaly promised. He would try, but he'd worked for Mr Cho for ten years and never once had his boss ever listened to anything he'd said. But he would try.

'More than a hundred years ago there was a young woman named Ah Ying. She was very beautiful. She lived beside the sea and was promised in marriage to a man she did not love. He was an old man, a merchant, but her family was poor and she was their only daughter. There was much money to be made by the arrangement.

'Ah Ying was unhappy at the approaching wedding. It was to take place when she was fourteen. One day, when she was at the seashore gathering shellfish, she looked up to see a boat approaching. On the boat were three fishermen from the nearby island. One of them, the youngest, was only twenty years old and he was very handsome. His name was Li Heng.

'Li Heng saw the beautiful young girl at the water's edge and his heart was immediately lost to her. So stunned was he by her beauty that for a moment he was lost. When the bow of the boat touched the sand, he overbalanced and tumbled into the water. His father and brother laughed at his misfortune but Ah Ying, seeing that he had cut his hand on a rock, went to his aid.

'When they touched, there was electricity between them, and it was love in the purest sense.' The old woman smiled, remembering a love that pure in her own youth. Ghazaly nodded. He had never felt love like that, but he had met others who had.

'Ah Ying tore a strip off her *samfoo* trousers to bind the young fisherman's wound. Li Heng's father and brother carried their water casks to the spring above the beach and filled them. When they returned, Ah Ying had finished her bandage.

'Li Heng's father cried out, "Say goodbye to your new

girlfriend. We have fish to catch." Li Heng didn't want to leave his new-found love but he was a fisherman. He went to the boat and helped push it back into deeper water. He raised his bandaged hand and could just make out the lone figure on the beach waving farewell. Li Heng kissed the bandage and waved the kiss to Ah Ying. She caught it and, smiling, gathered her basket of shellfish and started for home.

'Back at her village, Ah Ying's mother and aunts were gathered in their house. Ah Ying's fourteenth birthday was only two weeks away and the women were discussing the wedding. Ah Ying went to prepare dinner, her mind on the handsome young man she had just met. Suddenly there was a noise outside and Ah Ying could see her father chatting with the man she was about to marry.

'She peered at her husband-to-be from behind the curtain and started to cry. He didn't look any different since the last time she'd seen him. He was old, older than her father, and he was fat. He was balding with a scrawny beard and she knew that he smelled bad. He was so different from the beautiful young man on the beach.

'The next morning Ah Ying went to the beach but there was no sign of the fishing boat or the young man. The day after that and the day after that she went to the beach but still there was no sign of the young fisherman. With her heart almost breaking she resigned herself to the fact that she would never see him again.

'As the day of the wedding approached, Ah Ying decided that

she would rather take her own life than marry the pig of a man that she was betrothed to. With firm resolve she left her house in the early hours of the morning. She was wearing her best clothes and had her hair tied in a beautiful knot. On the beach she waited for the dawn and as the sun's rays touched the water, she stepped into the sea and began to walk, going deeper and deeper with every step.'

Ghazaly was enthralled by the tale. He was leaning closer and closer to the old woman as she talked. The lines on her face seemed to have lessened and she suddenly seemed so much younger than before.

'The water was almost as high as Ah Ying's neck when she saw it. Out of the morning sea mist came a small boat with a white sail and there, steering, was the handsome young man. He saw her in the water and came alongside, pulling down the sail and reaching out for her hand.

'Hours of pulling in heavy fishing nets had made Li Heng very strong. He lifted Ah Ying from the water as if she weighed nothing. He sat her in the bottom of the boat and began talking to her in a tongue she didn't understand. But they didn't need to understand. It was clear that love flowed between them.

'Suddenly there was an angry shout from the shore. It was Ah Ying's father and her older brother. When they saw Ah Ying in the boat with the stranger, all of their dreams of wealth turned to dust.

'Ah Ying took Li Heng's arm and begged him to sail away with her. Li Heng agreed and pulled up the sail. A strong breeze came from nowhere and soon they were gliding away across the water towards the island that was his home.

'When they arrived at Li Heng's village, he took Ah Ying to his brother's house. There his brother's wife looked after the girl. Both Li Heng's father and brother were fishing. He had told them he was ill so they had gone ahead without him.

'Several hours after they'd arrived at the village Li Heng saw the three boats heading their way. He immediately realised they were not from his village. It had to be the girl's father coming to claim her back.

'Quickly Li Heng found Ah Ying and together they ran into the jungle. All the men in Li Heng's village were out fishing so when the angry mob arrived, they were not stopped. They ran through the houses looking for Ah Ying. When they noticed the pathway into the jungle they followed it, wielding knives as they ran.

'Ah Ying also ran until she could run no longer. The mob was coming closer. Li Heng was prepared to fight but all he had was a fisherman's knife. He found a broken branch to make a cudgel but it was useless. There were too many of them.

'That was when Ah Ying began to pray. She prayed to her god to save them. Li Heng suddenly had an idea: she would hide and he would try to draw their pursuers away. Quickly he helped

Ah Ying into the branches of a tree. She managed to make herself small so she couldn't be seen. Li Heng ran off, shouting loudly to distract the mob.

'After a few moments Ah Ying could see her father, brother and the men they had gathered. They ran past the tree she was hiding in. Meanwhile Li Heng was running for his life, twisting and turning through the dense jungle. He didn't see the tree root that tripped him up, sending him crashing headfirst to the ground. Dazed and winded, he was unable to get up before the angry men were upon him.

'They swung their long knives and slashed and cut him until he was dead. The handsome young man was no more. His body lay lifeless on the ground.'

Ghazaly shuddered at this image. He had seen a man knifed to death once and the memory had never left him—it never would.

'The men from across the water found their way back to the village. Again they passed under the tree where Ah Ying was hiding. She pressed her body into the cool bark and waited until they had gone. Then she waited for Li Heng to come for her but he didn't. Finally she went to sleep.

'When she woke in the morning, Li Heng still hadn't come. She waited and waited until finally, her heart breaking, she died there in the arms of the Sanctuary Tree. No one ever found her body.' The old woman reached for the water bottle once more and took a large swig.

'This is the Sanctuary Tree,' she said, pointing to the thick trunk of the Bodhi. 'That is why it can never be cut down. That is why this temple was built here.'

Ghazaly looked up at the magnificent tree. It was so high. He could imagine that Ah Ying was still there, huddling in the branches, waiting for her fisherman to come for her.

'I will do my best to prevent Mr Cho from cutting it down,' he said. And he would. It might cost him his job, but he would try. 'I promise I will try,' he added, 'but he is a very greedy man.'

'Yes,' the old woman agreed, nodding her head sadly. 'Tell him that if he does cut it down, he will not live to enjoy the fruits of his old age.'

'I will, Old Mother.' Ghazaly looked up into the tree again and thought he could see the pretty face of the young girl peering down at him. He smiled at this fanciful idea and turned back to the old woman—but she wasn't there. He'd only seen her a few seconds before. She couldn't possibly have got up and walked away so quickly.

Ghazaly stood and looked all around him. The old woman was definitely not there and, furthermore, there was no sign she had ever been there. Even the soft earth bore no sign of her walking sticks. The foreman shook his head. He picked up the water bottle that sat on the masonry slab he had shared with the old lady, and walked past the Sanctuary Tree to where his truck was parked. Two labourers, who were supposed to be cutting down the Bodhi trees, were sitting smoking in the shade of another tree.

'We're leaving,' Ghazaly told the men. The pair of them climbed into the back of the truck and, without saying a word, the foreman started the engine. He would go to Mr Cho's office and tell him the story. Even if Mr Cho then decided to let him go, so be it. He would not be cutting down the trees or ordering anyone else to.

Ghazaly did indeed lose his job, but he quickly found another. Mr Cho hired another foreman and returned to the temple site. This foreman, Albert Hoong, was not a man given to fairy tales. He ordered the men to start cutting the largest tree first. The labourers switched on their chain saws and set to work.

After a few minutes, however, they had failed to make any progress cutting into the trunk of the Bodhi tree the old woman had named the Sanctuary Tree. The trunk just kept blunting the blades on the saws and the labourers had to keep stopping to sharpen them.

Mr Cho arrived at the site later that afternoon and when he saw that the biggest tree was still standing, he exploded with rage. Cursing and swearing, he stormed up to his foreman.

'Mr Hoong, why hasn't this damned tree been felled yet?'

'It's very large,' Mr Hoong explained. 'We have to keep stopping to sharpen the blades. It's nearly done.'

'Very well. Get on with it. I want it gone today!'

The foreman yelled at the men to get on with it. The man with the saw had just finished filing the blade and was preparing to start cutting again. The saw burst into life, smoking and howling. The man put the blade to the trunk and the teeth began to rip a huge gash in the wood. Another man started to hammer wedges into the gap as the saw continued to cut deeper and deeper. A broad crescent-shaped slice of wood fell away from the side of the trunk. This cut, the scarf cut, would be the one that determined which direction the tree would eventually fall.

In his youth Mr Cho had witnessed the felling of many trees. When he'd first set up his business, he had worked hard alongside his labourers. Now he was rich he didn't need to work. He stood to one side, well out of the way of the tree's intended path, and waited. He lit a cigar in anticipation of the celebration to come. When the temple and the trees were gone, the new condominiums would be built and he would add many millions to his already bulging bank account.

There was a loud shriek as strands of timber began to tear apart. The men at the base of the tree pulled the saw free and quickly stepped away from the trunk. The magnificent Bodhi began to fall exactly in the direction the scarf cut dictated it would.

'Good,' Mr Cho said through a haze of expensive cigar smoke. 'Very good.' With this tree gone, the others would soon follow.

However, as the magnificent tree began to gather momentum,

something went horribly wrong. Later, when asked what had happened, Mr Hoong and the labourers would all agree that it was as if a giant hand had grabbed the trunk of the falling tree and pushed it in a different direction.

Suddenly the cigar dropped from Mr Cho's mouth as he saw the huge trunk of the Bodhi swinging towards him. He tried to run but slipped on the mud. He tried to shout but no sound came. Within a split second tonnes of tree landed on him. Broken branches filled the air as the huge tree struck the ground with a loud boom, causing the foreman and his workmen to run for cover.

When the branches stopped flying and the dust and leaves settled, the foreman ran towards the spot where he had last seen his employer.

Immediately he stopped.

Protruding from under the trunk of the mighty Bodhi was one of Mr Cho's expensive shoes. That was when he knew that his boss would now be nothing more than a pulpy mess deep in the mud.

'Boss!' one of the labourers was calling from near the crown of the tree. 'Boss, look at this.'

Mr Hoong went to where the man was standing. There, where the crown of the tree had landed, was a small cluster of bones. Among the bones was a human skull.

'Boss,' the labourer said again. Mr Hoong looked to where

the man was pointing.

There, behind where Mr Cho's Mercedes was parked, stood an old lady. She was leaning on two sticks and staring at Mr Hoong and his men. The old lady shook her head and when Mr Hoong blinked, she was gone.

# The cell

'Please, let me out. It's time! It was only supposed to be for a week.'

Naked but for the thin grey blanket—the only item in the cell that wasn't fixed down—the young man lay huddled on his bunk, staring up at *it*.

*It* was the wide eye of the lens that stared blankly back at the prisoner from the Plexiglas turret in the centre of the high white ceiling. The camera was on a swivel mount. The mount also carried a motion sensor with a red diode. The diode flickered dully whenever the prisoner moved and the lens followed. There was nowhere to hide in the three-metre-by-three-metre cubicle that had been Kenny's home for the past three weeks.

The door, a vertical rectangle, had no hinges he could see and no handle or spy hole. It had been opened only once and that had been to admit him. He had agreed to one week but he was still here. That hadn't been in the disclaimer he had signed.

He had been recruited on campus to be part of an experiment into isolation and sleep deprivation. He had agreed because he needed the money and the payment of $1,000 was a lot of cash to a struggling student. The university, through its Behavioural

Psychology Unit, had endorsed the experiment. Kenny had been subjected to a physical and psychological profile test and pronounced fit, healthy and mentally stable. He had been the perfect candidate for the experiment. He was told he would be one of at least twenty subjects who would be tested over the coming months. He was to be the first.

The location of the cell was unknown to Kenny but he hadn't been that interested in anything other than the money, which had already been credited to his depleted bank account. Once he had signed on the dotted line, the three graduate students conducting the experiment had picked him up at his dormitory in a van. He had been told to bring nothing. They'd blindfolded him and when they'd eventually reached their destination, they'd made him strip naked before putting him into the cell.

'Welcome to Guantanamo Bay, Singapore style,' one of the students had quipped at him as they shut the door. That had been the last human voice Kenny had heard. Since he'd heard the sound of the heavy bolts being slammed home to secure the closed door, he'd sat alone in silence—total silence but for the muted whirring of the swivelling camera lens when he moved and the faint hum of the fan that pushed air into the cell.

Kenny lay motionless. He was playing a little game, able to defeat the sensor but not the camera lens. It remained locked in its position, waiting, watching. The cell he was in was white: the walls, the floor and the ceiling. It wasn't the gleaming white of an operating theatre. This was a dull, worn, waxy white, the colour of a fresh corpse. The only light came from a tube set in the ceiling to one side of the camera turret. The fluorescent glare was white, very bright and very white. It had never once been turned off and he had learned to sleep with it on, his face turned towards the wall.

The bed, long and narrow, was made from the same material as the walls and bonded to it. There was no gap underneath and the mattress and pillow were one, a thin layer of foam rubber covered in a plastic film. Even this was fixed to the contoured base of the bed. The only other furniture in the room was a toilet pan that protruded from the wall opposite the bunk. The pan was made from the same kind of white fibreglass or plastic as the bunk and the cell walls. There was no seat to raise, lower or tear off and use to attack the walls or the camera in its high turret. On the wall above the toilet was a flush button. Paper was dispensed through a covered slot in the wall. It was shiny, non-absorbent and totally unsuitable for its purpose.

The floor around the toilet sloped to a drain by the wall. The shower fitting was set in the ceiling above. There was another button in the wall under it. There were no taps to adjust the water temperature, not that it would have made any difference. The water was always cold, icy cold, and the smell of chlorine was strong. There was no soap and no towel. Kenny had used his blanket to dry himself only once. He had then had to curl up in his damp blanket and shiver away a long night—if it had been night. He had no real way of knowing what time of day it was.

The cell wasn't cold though. The temperature never changed. The air that blew in through the grate above the door was always warm. It smelt of rubber and oil but it seemed stale and depleted of oxygen.

Kenny lay looking up at the camera. He played games with it because it was all he had, his only link to the world outside and his captors. Sometimes, often, it was almost a friend. And as friends do, he teased it, taunted it, directed all his failing passion and anger at it. He shouted obscenities at it and whispered to it, cried to it.

Kenny knew the term 'Stockholm Syndrome' and he realised that he had succumbed to it. He loved the camera as much as he hated its cold, impersonal eye. No matter what he said or did it stared back at him, unblinking, playing its own game. He always blinked first and turned away because it never blinked. It never betrayed any of the emotions he directed at it. Just once he wanted to see something, a spark of compassion, anger even. Anything but the cold circle of glass that bore down on him so relentlessly.

He had been lying motionless for an hour, maybe two. Not entirely motionless; under the blankets he played another game. Using the overgrown nail of his right thumb, he was carving yet another faint nick into the edge of his bunk frame. This was telling him how long he had been in this place. To tell what time of the day it was had been impossible at first. There was no night, no day in the cell. How long it had taken him to work out a way of keeping track of his days and the time frame of each individual day, he didn't know. Possibly two or three days in total. In the end it had been his own body that had given him the answer.

Ever since childhood, Kenny had always been regular at his toilet. At 7 am, no matter what sort of night he'd had, his body drove him to the toilet. When he defined that memory, he used his own body clock to measure his days. He would go to the toilet, wash his hands under the cold water of the shower then return to his blanket and his bunk. There, hidden, careful not to betray his movements, he would patiently pick at the hard plastic until he'd carved another groove with his fingernail. Every day, when he had completed a new mark, he would lie and count them. Today there were twenty-two grooves in the hard plastic. He'd been there one day over three weeks, and perhaps one or two more as well.

'Please let me out!' Kenny sat up suddenly. He suddenly remembered Chelsea. He hadn't told her about his week as part of the experiment and anyway, she had been visiting friends in Kuantan. Now she would be back, wondering where he was. They were almost engaged.

Had anyone else missed him? What about his friends, his fellow students? His parents were both elderly and now lived quietly in Punggol. Kenny was the youngest of five siblings. He had little contact with his parents other than the occasional phone call and a monthly visit. Things had not been good between them due to some silliness on his part. It had been an incident involving alcohol and several fellow students. It had been reported in the newspapers and Kenny and his fellows had come very close to being expelled from the university.

'You have shamed the family name,' his father had told him at the time and their relationship had become very strained. But what about his brothers and sisters? Had they asked about him? Had they gone looking for him? Did they think he had had an accident, run away or even committed suicide?

'Why have you kept me so long?' Kenny yelled in frustration. He climbed off the bed and began stalking around the cell. The camera above whirred as it tried to keep up with his frantic pacing. Eventually he tired and sat down on his bunk again. He had spent many hours doing just that, alternately pacing then sitting, babbling and begging to be released, begging for a reaction of any sort. It never came. Only when he stood and began pacing did he hear the sound of the camera's guidance mechanism. In a perverse way, the whirring of its servo as it tracked him had become a comforting sound. He changed direction several times in one circuit of the cell, forcing the camera to dart backwards and forwards. It was a petty thing to do but somehow it helped keep him sane—if indeed he was sane. He wasn't sure anymore.

'Food!' he muttered, knowing that soon the floor-level slot in the wall beside the door would open and the mechanism outside would push in a tray. His meal would be the same as always: a small bottle of water, a sealed foil packet of cold vegetable gruel, a packet of cold soft noodles, a piece of processed cheese and six rice crackers. Everything was vacuum-sealed. This was food that would never spoil and never taste of anything much. There was a plastic spoon on the tray for him to eat with. That was it. It never varied. How he longed for a change. He had had dreams of chicken rice, *char kway teow*, beers and ice cream, litres of it.

There was a clank and a white plastic tray slid across the floor. A transparent film was bonded across, and beneath it Kenny saw his meal. It was the same as always. He stood up and, leaving his blanket where it fell, he moved to where the food lay. He retrieved the tray and sat back on his bunk. Once, he'd tried peering out through the gap but there was nothing to see, just the metal bars of the mechanism.

Why can't I see anyone? Why can't I hear them? Those questions had plagued him from the beginning. Now they rarely entered his mind.

The first day he had kept his tray and the debris from his meal, waiting for someone to come and take it from him. He'd wanted to see his captors. No one came. He hung on and on, realising that a couple of days must have gone by. No more food arrived, and the slot through which the tray had arrived remained open, a black slash at floor level. Eventually he had taken his tray and pushed it back through the slot. There had been the sound of a mechanism at work then the slot had closed. Perhaps it was their way of punishing him, he would never know, but the next food tray had been a long time coming. After that he'd stopped playing that particular game. He would take his tray, eat his food, drink his water and push the tray back into the slot. It became a ritual, one that seemed to guarantee he would be fed the next time.

Seated on his bunk, Kenny sipped his water. Water was not a problem really. There was water in the shower if he needed it, the toilet even, but that had a chemical cleaning agent in it. It would scour his insides as it did the toilet bowl. First he ate the gruel with the soft noodles, then he ate the cheese with the crackers. Lastly he swallowed the remaining water. It was lukewarm and tasted stale, as always. Meal finished, he loaded everything onto the tray and went to the hole in the wall, squatting to push the tray through. The hole closed and he could just make out the faint sound of a machine as his rubbish was carried away.

Back on his bunk, the prisoner draped his blanket around his shoulders and stared up at the camera lens.

'When is this going to be over?' he asked. 'I only signed on for a week.' He leaned forward then quickly sat back. He saw the focus of the lens change. The red light of the sensor flared. The prisoner almost smiled through the straggly beard that was growing on his previously smooth cheeks. 'Who is the prisoner? You or me?' he whispered. He had begun talking to the camera after three or four days. Doubtless there was a microphone attached to the mechanism. No matter what his captors saw on screen, all he saw from his side was an eye. It was a mechanical eye but it moved, it changed in subtle ways and he controlled it. It couldn't and it didn't control him. In a way it had almost become some sort of dumb pet. He moved, it moved. That had led to his main source of entertainment.

Kenny often wondered if he could cause it to break down, to malfunction in some way. Then they would have to come and fix it. They would have no choice because without the camera their experiment would fail. But no matter how long he forced himself to move around his prison—changing direction and speed, goading it into its sluggish action, the mechanism whining and humming—he eventually had to stop. It won, as it always did.

He started to cry. He was crying more and more often. The frustration, the loneliness, the uncertainty, it was all devouring him.

'Let me *out*!' he screamed, tears coursing down his cheeks, running through his sparse whiskers and dropping to the floor. 'Please?' he whimpered. Then his mood changed, as it always did, reverting back to anger. 'It's over you bastards. It's over. Let me go!' Anger, frustration, they intermingled in equal parts. But as always the outburst was short. He was too tired, too beaten physically and mentally for anger. The days and nights had worn him down in every way. Once a chubby ninety kilos, he now doubted if he weighed seventy-five.

So Kenny sat cross-legged on his bunk with the blanket draped around his shoulders. He closed his eyes. He had tried meditation at one time, now he was trying to relearn the lessons. He began his breathing. This was one way he could escape. The camera was locked on the motionless man. The diode in the sensor was still. Kenny left his white cell and tried to set his mind free.

'Four weeks,' he said. Kenny had been in the cell for four weeks and still nothing but him and the camera. But things were different. Today there was no food tray. He had had to use water from the shower for drinking and that puzzled him. Usually the pressure in the shower was strong, but not today. The water was little more than a trickle.

'What is happening?' Kenny asked the question but his friend in the ceiling remained silent. The only sound was the flexing of the lens whenever he moved and the flicker of the sensor. 'How much longer?' The tears had started again. He was crying more and more now as frustration ate at his soul. 'How much longer?'

Kenny closed his eyes and ignored the glare of the white fluorescent tube that still burned its way through his eyelids. He had learned to sleep this way. Sleep and meditation were his only escape. In his dreams he could be with Chelsea and his friends. Sometimes it was so real. But always he would wake up to his nightmare and often he would scream, shriek and curse the unseen, begging them to let him go.

No food. It hadn't come for a second day. There was the clank of the mechanism and the slot opened, but no tray appeared. Was he being punished? If so, why? He hadn't done anything. *Couldn't* do anything. The prisoner was sitting on his bunk, staring at the place where the tray would normally appear—*should* have appeared.

'Why?' he mumbled the words and stared up at the camera. It was staring back. He stood and began pacing. Kenny had done two complete circuits of his cell when he realised that something was wrong. There was no sound of the camera moving. He stopped and looked up at the turret. The camera lens was still fixed on his bed, the place where he had been.

'Friend, what ails you?' he asked as he moved to stand between the camera and the bunk, but there was no sound from above. The diode from the sensor didn't flash red. The prisoner raised a hand and waved it across the face of the lens. No red blur, no whining mechanism. 'Damn!' Kenny lowered his hand and sat heavily on the bunk, his head spinning with the implications of it all. If the camera was broken, they would have to come and fix it. He was about to meet those who had put him there. What would he say? Would he rant, rave, scream and curse, or would he meekly ask them to let him go, to honour the agreement he had signed? Compensation, he would ask for compensation, he would . . .

He sat on his bunk staring up at the camera, almost willing the sensor light to come on, almost wanting to hear the mechanism clunk and whirr again. It didn't happen. The lens stared down at him, blank, dead. He moved his hand. Nothing. 'Dead!' he whispered as if mourning an old friend. It had always been there for him. It had always moved when he had. It had supplied virtually the only sound, the only movement in this place, apart from when his food arrived. He had often flushed the toilet or turned on the shower just for the effect, for any movement and noise to break the monotony. There had never once been a fly, a spider, a mouse or a moth to distract him, not once in all those days.

In a way he had come to totally rely on the eye in the roof. He knew it was an unintentional pun, but the camera had become the focus of his existence. He abused it in his anger, cried at it in his loneliness and frustration, sang to it, talked to it. In a way, it alone had stopped him slipping over the edge into complete madness.

Kenny stood and completed a circuit of his cage. Still no sound, no movement from above. 'Oh,' he said softly, helplessly sinking back to his bed. Where were they, the three who had created this prison? Why hadn't they released him? Surely the experiment was over. Or had it just begun? That thought started

Kenny pacing again. Perhaps this was the real experiment. The week of confinement had just been the bait to lure him into their trap and their diabolical mind game.

Another day passed and still they hadn't come to repair the camera. The mechanism that used to feed him whirred and clanged but no food arrived. Kenny was hungry, far hungrier than he had ever been in his other life.

'Where are you?' he shouted. He had been shouting those three words over and over and his throat was sore, his voice hoarse. The white walls killed even the faintest echo. Kenny sat for an hour, two, he had no idea how long. Then, with no warning, the fluorescent light flickered and died and the faint hum from the fan faded. He was alone in the dark and the silence. 'No!' he screamed. He scrambled to his feet and groped in the darkness, finding the button that activated the shower. He pushed the button but there was nothing. The trickle he had been drinking from, the only thing that was keeping him alive, was gone. There was no water. Kenny groped along the wall to the toilet control. He hesitated then pushed the flush mechanism. The water swirled, gurgled and was gone, but no more flowed into the pan.

'What's happening?' the prisoner screamed as he stood there in the blackness. 'What's going on?' He was shouting now, turning to face the door, waiting for them to appear. But they didn't come for him. Not this day.

Another day passed and thirst was the first thing to get to him—that and the smell of the foul slime his bowels had begun to give out. It lay in the toilet bowel, its stench filling the still air.

'Why?' That one word that had been with him for so long had now taken on a new meaning. 'Why? Why? Why?' He repeated it over and over again. Were they going to let him die of dehydration and starvation? Leave his body to rot where it fell?

'*Why*?' In the stinking blackness the naked, filthy, stick-thin man continued to shout as he paced, or rather staggered, around his cell. He shouted and staggered, staggered and shouted. To stop was maybe to cease moving forever and die.

What made him go to the cell door? Kenny would never know. Perhaps he'd stumbled towards it. Perhaps he'd meant to touch it—but touch it he did. He slammed against it in the darkness and it opened.

Kenny stood staring at the white crack that had appeared in his black world.

'Open!' he whispered. 'Open!' He stood frozen, unbelieving. 'Open!' he repeated for the third time, his mind overwhelmed by the implications. Were they outside waiting for him to emerge? He stood by the gap in the door for a minute, two, ten, he had no idea. It was no more than ten centimetres wide. Finally he turned away from the spectre of freedom and, using the pale light to guide him, he went and sat on his bed. He gathered the blanket around his shoulders and sat staring at the door. More time passed. There was no sound from outside, no movement. His looked up at the ceiling and the camera. He could just make out the turret. There was no diode and he knew that the lens was staring blankly down at him.

'What's happening?' he asked it in a voice barely above a whisper. 'Please, what's happening?' He was pleading now, but he received no sign that anyone could hear him. He raised a hand but the diode on the sensor remained dead. 'Oh God!' He dropped his hand. 'What is happening?'

The prisoner sat waiting, motionless, a skin-and-bone skeleton. He was frozen but for his darting eyes and the throbbing pulse in his neck. His breathing was so shallow that the accordion of his protruding ribs barely moved.

'Go!' a voice inside was telling him. 'Go! Leave!' It was Chelsea's voice, the voice of his dreams. 'If I try to go they might kill me,' he said out loud.

'If you stay you are dead!' The voice countered with the simple truth. Kenny stood up, holding the blanket close. He went over to the door and stood, slowly turning to look up at the ceiling, squinting in the half-light. The lens hadn't followed him. 'I'm going now!' he said. 'I'm leaving!' As he had suspected, there was no reply. The camera was dead and he was alive. With a trembling hand he pushed the door and flinched as it swung wide open, effortlessly, silently. He stepped into the light.

The warehouse was enormous and it was light. Unlike the fluorescent light in his cell, this light was brown, filtering through transparent sheets in the roof. Diffused it may have been, but it reached down and touched everything. Kenny immediately noticed that the warehouse was silent and deserted. He turned back to face the cell where he had been held captive for so long. For the first time he could see the mechanism that had fed him. There was a magazine and a tall rack above it. The rack was empty. A small electric motor was attached to the mechanism to work the slide to push the trays in and retrieve them. A dozen empty trays lay to one side. Someone was supposed to come and fill the magazine but they hadn't been for a long time. There were unopened boxes of food stacked beside the mechanism. They had said that the experiment would be going on for a year and many volunteers would be involved. That was all very well, but why had they stopped feeding him? Kenny noticed a tank above the cell with a hose running into it. The tank fed the toilet and the shower. Why had they not filled the tank? Why had the camera and the light shut down and he'd almost run out of air?

'Why?' he asked, knowing the answer already. The machine had dispensed his food at exactly the same time each day. He suspected there had been no one here for weeks—no one but himself. He moved around the outside of his cell, stepping over the timber braces that were holding up the walls. It had seemed so solid inside, but outside it was like a movie set. Thick insulation blocked out sound and rubber hoses ran from one wall of the cell to the shadows beyond. They must have carried his toilet and water waste. Another rack on the wall was stacked with sheets of toilet paper. Everything was set up to be self-sufficient for long periods of time.

'Why did you stop feeding me?' Kenny asked, clutching his blanket around his shoulders. He'd completed his circuit of the cell and was now standing back at the front door and the food-supply mechanism. Its frame made a ladder. Slowly he climbed it until he was level with the roof. He had enough light to see what he needed to. There, in the centre of the room, sat his camera. Kenny pulled himself onto the roof and half-crawled, half-walked to the centre.

The camera was housed in a box. A series of cables linked it to a bank of car batteries but there were no other wires that Kenny could see, no signal-feed wires, no antenna. The realisation hit him like a punch to the gut. He fell back on his haunches then collapsed onto his knees. The camera had been nothing but a dummy. Everything he had done, everything he had said, no one had heard, no one had seen.

'Why?' he shouted as he stood shakily, the blanket falling to his feet. 'Why? Why?' He was screaming now, a long keening wail of despair that echoed back from the walls of the dusty, brown cavern. Kenny turned and scrambled down to the warehouse floor, almost falling down the scaffolding as he went.

Then he saw it.

'How could I have missed it?' he whispered. There, positioned so anyone emerging from the cell would see it, was a table. On the table was a computer and a counter, a simple scoring mechanism with large numerals. Because there was no electricity supply the counter had frozen on the number fifty-three. Above the counter was a sign. Kenny moved closer to read it.

*Congratulations. You have been a prisoner in a cell with an unlocked door for the number of days shown below. Please use the mobile phone on the table to call us and we will come and collect you. The phone is configured to only call one number. Thank you Prisoner No. 1, you will be compensated for any additional days over your contracted time.*

*Vincent Chua, Philip Lim and Roger Lau of the Psychological Deprivation Experiment Team, Behavioural Psychology Department, University of Singapore.*

'No!' he shouted. 'Oh, no!' All along the door hadn't been locked. He had never thrown himself at it, beaten his fists on it, shoved his body at it. All along, from the moment it had been closed with the sound of heavy sliding bolts, he had assumed it was impossible to open. And, despite his desperation, he'd never even tried.

That was when he saw the CD player sitting next to the counter. 'Sound effects,' he mumbled, turning to look at the door. It was just plastic. Simple spring clips, one at the top and one at the bottom, had held it closed. Just a small amount of pressure would have opened it. With shaking hands Kenny switched on the mobile phone and pushed the green button.

'I'm sorry. The number you are calling is switched off or disconnected. Pease try again later. I'm sorry, the number you are calling is switched off or disconnected. Please try again later. I'm sorry . . .' Kenny let out an almighty scream.

Chris Yu had just finished loading his truck. He was leaning on the flank of his Isuzu enjoying a cigarette while Tan Thean Loon, the warehouse manager, completed the paperwork. The industrial estate in Jurong had a dozen or so units, each leased privately for different purposes.

Suddenly Chris stopped. The sound coming from a warehouse a hundred metres away sounded like a man yelling. He turned to look at the unit just as Mr Tan was coming towards him, holding a clipboard and a stack of papers which he handed to Chris.

'Sounds as if someone's got a problem,' he said, motioning towards the warehouse. The warehouse manager shrugged.

'Everyone's got a problem,' he replied. 'That place is off limits. Some sort of experiment run by the university. Only three people are allowed in. I haven't seen anyone for weeks, but they have leased it for a year. The electricity was disconnected a while ago because they haven't paid the account. I presume someone will be along to sort that out but it's not our business.'

'Okay,' Chris agreed. He had three more deliveries to make and was already running late. He swung up into the cab. The truck's big diesel engine drowned out the screams from the warehouse. As the gears ground into action, Chris rolled away. He waved at Mr Tan as he turned towards the gate.

Thean Loon watched the truck until it was out of sight. The noise from the other building had stopped. He shrugged and headed for his office. Whatever was going on wasn't any of his business.

In his cluttered office, the manager shook his head. He was responsible for the day shift, Glen Phua the night. Glen was messy and there were food containers and newspapers everywhere. According to Glen, the night shift was boring and reading alleviated his boredom.

Thean Loon gathered an armful of newspapers and dumped them in the rubbish bin by the door, pausing momentarily to look at the front page of the topmost paper.

The headline read: PROMISING YOUNG RESEARCHERS KILLED IN FREAK ACCIDENT. He looked at the photographs and recognised at least one of the young men. He'd seen him right there, at the warehouse leased by the university. Curious, Thean Loon read the whole article.

*Vincent Chua, Philip Lim and Roger Lau of the Behavioural Psychology Department at NUS were killed when the van they were driving was involved in a collision with truck on Boon Lay Way. The truck driver was also killed in the resulting fire.*

'Unlucky,' he muttered. He glanced at the date. It had happened three weeks ago. 'Very unlucky,' he repeated, shutting the lid on the bin and going back into the office. 'No doubt,' he thought, 'someone will come one day to sort out the warehouse.'

Kenny had opened a box of pre-packaged food and was devouring his second tray, washing everything down with bottled water. He had filled the water tank on the roof of the cell. The power to the warehouse was switched off but as long as there was light during the day and he slept at night, he would be fine. He had food to last forever. He raised the mobile phone to his ear.

'I'm sorry. The number you are calling is switched off or disconnected. Please try again later. I'm sorry, the number you are calling is switched off or disconnected. Please try again later. I'm sorry . . .'

'Someone will come one day,' Kenny said, putting the phone down. 'One day!' He pulled his blanket close around his shoulders as he lay on his bunk. 'One day!'

# A long life

'You will live for a very long time!' The sharp, yellow talon which was tracing the lines on Adrian Choo's palm tickled him as it moved. Then it stopped, hesitating, before continuing to move across his palm, retracing its path to pause where the deepest of the fate lines bisected the long curve of the lifeline.

'A very long time!' the fortune-teller repeated, but this time Adrian could see a shadow had crept across her face. Her thin lips were pursed either in thought or recognition, and for just a single heartbeat, the faintest of furrows touched her brow.

'A long life?' Adrian echoed, wanting much more, needing to hear those magic words of 'happy, healthy, rich, successful' but they were not offered. The old woman's eyes reluctantly met his for a moment, then slid away.

'You will live for a very long time!' Her hands came together. The long thin fingers were agitated, moving as if they had a life of their own. Adrian began to feel uneasy. Her fingers were scuttling and twitching like spiders—and he hated spiders.

Laughter outside broke the tension and he glared. This drunken dare to have his fortune told was supposed to have been fun. He heard Benson, Jin Chou and the girls outside giggling through the thin curtain that separated him from the evening bustle of Chinatown.

'Is there more?' Adrian turned to the fortune-teller, sensing there was.

'That is all I see,' replied the woman. She delivered her lie convincingly, but something in her dark eyes gave her away. Adrian stood up. He laid the ten-dollar note on the table and anchored it with his fingers. One of the old woman's hands fluttered towards the note only to retreat like a confused bird when he made no move to release it.

'A long and happy life?' he repeated, desperate now to hear those words from her lips.

'You will live to a great age,' she whispered, 'a great age.'

'How long?' Adrian almost shouted in his frustration. For a moment the woman hesitated. There was silence. Adrian tensed. Finally she replied.

'You will live to be ninety-eight years old.'

'Ninety-eight!' he shouted, stunned. Adrian's eyes searched her face for another lie, but there was none. The bland mask had been replaced with a face full of pity.

'Yes,' she said sadly, 'ninety-eight.'

Adrian turned and rejoined his grinning friends outside.

'So?' Benson quizzed him immediately.

'I'll tell you over food,' Adrian replied, grabbing his friend by the arm. 'Come on, let's go to VivoCity to meet the others.' The group of friends headed for the MRT.

That was in 2007. Adrian Choo was twenty-seven years old. According to the old woman, he would live until the year 2078.

Today is 3 July 2020. It is Adrian's birthday. He is forty.

I have fifty-eight more years to live, he thinks and starts to cry.

Adrian cannot speak or move any part of his body other than his eyes. He has been like this since that night in 2007 when a car struck him as he staggered across Telok Blangah Road after a night out with his friends at VivoCity. Now, thirteen years after his world crashed around him, machines breathe for him and tubes feed him. Fifty-eight more years of *this*! he silently cries.

Violet, Adrian's caregiver, gently wipes away his tears with a tissue. She does this frequently because Adrian cries often. Violet smiles encouragement and moves away. She can't hear Adrian screaming inside. The only sounds in the room are the wheezing of the respirator and the happy beeping of the heart monitor, signaling to Adrian that he is still alive.

# Encounter with Grandma

I was born in Hong Kong and it was there I met Philip, my future husband. Philip was Singaporean and he was in Hong Kong on a one-year transfer with his company.

When he returned to Singapore, we dated long distance for two years before we married and I moved to Singapore to be with him.

At first things were good but Philip drank a lot and liked to gamble. Things between us started to sour in our second year of marriage. At the end of that year I gave birth to twin boys, and after that Philip started to become violent. Sometimes I feared for the children.

Then the police became involved and my brothers came from Hong Kong to speak to Philip. Shortly afterwards he left us and got a company transfer to Bangkok. He never came back and I applied for a divorce.

When I met Kelvin, I'd been a single mum for five very long, very lonely years. Kelvin seemed like a really nice guy. He was a manager at one of the hotels on Sentosa. He was a good-looking man and very attentive to me. He provided me with everything that a lonely woman, haunted by memories of a bad marriage, could ever wish for.

I fell very much in love with Kelvin and because he came from a wealthy family and had a very good job, he had a nice apartment in Bukit Timah. My divorce had just come through, and I was looking forward to eventually marrying him. The boys liked him and already regarded him as their new dad.

One holiday we all went to Hong Kong to see my family. My grandmother, who was ninety-two, was in failing health and I wanted her and the rest of the family to meet Kelvin to see if they approved of him. After Philip I was perhaps doubting my own intuition and my ability to judge men.

At our family home in Aberdeen, my father and mother made us all welcome. The bad news was that Grandma was in hospital with breathing problems. I went to see her first with the boys. She was in bed in a single room, propped up on pillows. There were oxygen tubes in her nose but, despite everything, she was as alert as always. After we'd greeted each other and talked for a while, she wanted to know where Kelvin was. I told her that I would bring him to visit the next day.

The next day at visiting time Kelvin and I walked into Grandma's room. She and Kelvin talked a lot and I could see that she liked him. However just when we were about to leave, Grandma shot him a fierce look which was very unlike her.

'You look after Michelle, young man. When I die, which will

be soon, I will be looking down on you both. I don't want her to be unhappy. If you mistreat her, you will have to answer to me.'

Kelvin looked surprised and I must admit I felt that way too. Later we discussed what she had said. I was touched by her concern but we moved on, and the warning from Grandma was soon forgotten.

The rest of the holiday went well and we returned to Singapore. We had a small wedding three weeks later. Mother, Father and my brothers came down from Hong Kong to attend. It was a beautiful day and I was very content.

After we'd been married only a few months Kelvin's company began having severe financial difficulties. The hotel was sold. Suddenly Kelvin was out of work and he didn't take it well. Like Philip before him, he started to drink. Every job he applied for either required someone with fewer qualifications or the pay simply wasn't good. We were fortunate that the apartment was owned by his family and fully paid for.

Grandma died just a few weeks after Kelvin lost his job and I flew back to Hong Kong by myself for the funeral. Kelvin and I couldn't both afford to go, and given the angry and frustrated mood Kelvin was in, I didn't think it was a good idea anyway. So I went alone and he stayed and looked after the boys, who were both at school.

When I returned from Hong Kong, I took a taxi home

from Changi Airport. When I walked into the apartment, I was astounded. The place was a mess. Kelvin was sitting watching television with a bottle of whisky. He'd never drunk whisky before. It was the middle of the day and the boys were at school.

I scolded him severely. I told him that he needed to stop feeling sorry for himself. That was when he hit me. With my nose bleeding, I ran into our bedroom and locked the door. I felt terrible, not so much from the pain of the slap but from the fact that it was happening all over again, just like it had happened with Philip.

I couldn't help thinking that I was to blame, that it was all my fault. Did I attract men like Philip just so they could abuse me? I curled up on the bed and sobbed myself to sleep. Kelvin knocked on the door several times, asking me to let him in. I just ignored him.

When my boys came home from school, I just wanted to go and hug them, but I didn't want them to see my bruised face. I heard Kelvin tell them that Mummy was sick and that they would see me in the morning.

So I just lay on my bed, feeling miserable. Kelvin looked after the boys. He fed them, helped them with their homework then put them to bed. Eventually the apartment fell silent. After a few moments there was a faint knock on the bedroom door.

'Can I come in? I'm so sorry for what I did,' Kelvin whispered, but I could hear the sorrow in his voice plainly enough. I got off the bed and opened the door. He tentatively tried to hug me but I wasn't ready for that yet. Later in bed I let him put his arms around me. He lay there whispering about how he would try to get himself together, how he would get whatever job came up next in order to have some money coming in.

Eventually we went to sleep. I was still hurting inside, but I had decided that we had to make our marriage work so I would not be nasty and I would try very hard to support him.

It was just a few minutes after 2 am when I woke with a start. I could hear a strange noise and for a moment I couldn't place it. Then I realised that is was coming from Kelvin. He was lying beside me and seemed to be struggling to breathe. I turned on the bedside light to see my husband lying flat on his back. He seemed to be struggling to push something off his chest but there was nothing there. I helped him sit up. He was gasping for air, pale, sweating and in great distress. Suddenly he gave a huge shudder and started breathing deeply.

'What's wrong?' I asked, panic-stricken. He reached for the water bottle he kept by the bed and drank greedily from it. He was shaking and it took him several minutes to settle enough to tell me.

'I had a dream,' he said. 'I think it was a dream. There was a weight on my chest and when I opened my eyes to see what it was, I saw your grandmother. She was just sitting on me, sitting staring down at me with *that look* on her face. I couldn't move her and every time I tried, she seemed to get heavier and heavier. I don't know if I was awake or dreaming. She just sat there suffocating me. Then she said, "Look after Michelle," and vanished.'

Kelvin and I didn't go back to sleep that night. We talked and talked and in the morning, before the boys awoke, he went out. When he came back he had a copy of *The Straits Times*, a big bunch of flowers and a card for me saying how sorry he was.

Whether it was Grandma's influence or not, Kelvin got the next job he applied for. It was the position of assistant manager for one of Singapore's best hotels. Now, three years later, everything is fantastic between us. Kelvin no longer drinks any alcohol. We never quarrel. The boys love Kelvin and I am happy.

Thank you, Grandma!

# Tears of the rain tree

'It was planted by your great grandfather. You can't cut it down!'

'The farm is mine, therefore the tree is mine,' Ahmad firmly stated.

'But it is a beautiful tree,' protested Aishah, Ahmad's mother.

'I farm ducks, not trees. If I cut it down, I can build a new shed on the land—and I need the shed more than I need a stupid rain tree.'

'But it's part of our family history. When your great grandfather came here and bought the land, he planted the tree. It was one of the first Golden Rain Trees in Singapore.'

'It only looks golden. If it really was made of gold, I wouldn't need to build another shed. I wouldn't need to farm ducks,' Ahmad replied.

'Your great grandfather's spirit will not be happy with you.'

'I don't believe in all that superstitious nonsense. I am a modern man. I don't want to live in the past. The tree is part of the past.' With that he stormed out of the house. Aishah went to the window and watched her son drive away. The farm was small, she knew that. She also knew that they needed more land, but this was Singapore. There was no more land, at least land that they could afford. They couldn't compete with the property developers. She looked across at the sheds that housed the ducks. There, behind the sheds, along the boundary with their neighbours, the Choy family, was the rain tree.

It was a beautiful tree. It formed a broad canopy and that was the problem—the spreading branches provided shade to such a large area. Aishah sighed again. Her son had always been headstrong. She had four children, but Ahmad was her only son, so when his father died he naturally inherited the farm. She was old and tired, and she knew that she couldn't argue with him any more. Besides, Ahmad wasn't listening.

Aishah went to make some tea to calm her nerves. Ahmad would soon return. She suspected he had gone to borrow or rent an electric saw so he could cut down the tree. With a heavy sigh she made her tea and, taking her cup with her, she went outside, past the sheds and down to the rain tree. It was another hot day so she perched on the log bench under the tree, its wide canopy protecting her from the midday sun. The bench had been made many years ago by her late husband, Faizal. This was where he used to come to sit and think. Sometimes she would join him.

Aishah had been there for only a few minutes when she realised that droplets of water were falling from the leaves of the rain tree. She looked up, but the sky above was still bright—there was no rain. She knew that at night the leaves would close up to allow falling rain to reach the crown, but during the day it was very unlikely. So where were the rain droplets coming from?

'Are you crying?' she asked softly. There was, of course, no answer, but she could've sworn the rain was falling heavier now, dampening her *baju kurong*.

'I can't let him cut you down,' she said at last. 'I must make him see sense.' With that, Aishah stood up and walked back to the house. She was almost at the door when she realised she had left her cup behind. Never mind. She would collect it later. Now she had to make her stubborn son see sense.

Ahmad arrived home. In the back of his van was a petrol-driven chain saw. He had never used such a saw before, but his friend had given him a quick lesson. It seemed simple enough. As he got out of his van he paused. He knew that if he went back into the house, his mother would start to argue with him again. His mind was made up. He took the chain saw and set off towards the rain tree.

'Ahmad?' his mother called from the house. He gave her a dismissive wave and kept walking. 'Please, Ahmad, please don't cut the tree down. It's crying, Ahmad,' she shouted.

'Crying,' he muttered to himself. 'Now the tree is crying. She's losing her mind.' He soon arrived at the tree and, knowing his mother wouldn't be far behind, he quickly set up the chain saw. Suddenly it started to rain. Ahmad frowned and looked up. Raindrops were falling onto his upturned face, yet the sky was clear and bright.

'My imagination,' he snorted as he took hold of the handle to start the saw.

'Don't, Ahmad, please!'

'It has to go,' he shouted back, seeing his mother running towards him. 'It has to come down.' The rain was falling heavily now. His hair was slicked to his head and his shirt was sodden. 'What the hell is going on?' he cried, and walked out from under the canopy of the rain tree. Once he was out of its protective covering, the rain stopped.

Ahmad put the saw on the ground, placed his foot where his friend had shown him and pulled the cord to start it. The chain saw roared into life, spluttering and crackling. Grinning, Ahmad went back under the tree's canopy but again the rain began to fall heavily. Ignoring the freakish weather, he positioned the saw on the tree and proceeded to make the first cut. All of sudden the chain saw spluttered and died.

With a grunt of frustration he pulled the cord again. The saw spluttered but didn't start. He tried again. Once more the saw spluttered but refused to start. Ahmad tried to start the saw a third time, but failed.

By now he was soaking wet. He walked back out from under the tree. His mother stood to one side. She didn't say anything, but was looking at the tree in amazement. The tree really was crying.

Determined, Ahmad tried the saw again. This time it started immediately, buzzing into life.

'This time the tree *will* come down,' he stated as he once more advanced towards its trunk. But again, just as he positioned the saw, ready to make the first cut, it coughed and died. Ahmad was furious, his anger turning to rage.

'Look,' his mother was saying. 'The tree is crying because it wants to be saved. Please, in the memory of your father, your grandfather and your great grandfather, please don't cut it down.'

'I need the land to build another shed,' Ahmad snapped, marching away with the chain saw. 'I'm going to get my axe. That will definitely work!'

'Please,' his mother pleaded, but he ignored her. The axe was in a shed by the back door of the house. Ahmad put down the chain saw, picked up the axe and strode back to the rain tree. His mother was sobbing quietly. She didn't know what else to do and the tears from the tree were still falling.

Ahmad stood beside the trunk of the rain tree. He raised his axe and drove it towards the wood. The axe struck the tree, but it didn't make a cut. Instead it deflected off the trunk, twisted around in Ahmad's hand like a serpent, then embedded itself in his shin. At first he was so shocked by what he had just witnessed that the pain didn't hit home. Only when he looked down and saw the bloody mess did he begin to cry out in agony. The head of the axe was stuck firmly in his leg.

'Oh my goodness!' Aishah screamed. 'Oh my goodness!'

'Please, Mak, get help!' Ahmad sank onto the log bench under the tree. The rain had suddenly stopped. He stared at the axe. There was blood on his trousers but as yet no terrible crimson fountain had sprung up from the wound.

'Don't touch it,' his mother ordered. 'If you pull it out, it will bleed terribly. I will call the ambulance.' With that she hurried away.

Pale-faced and in shock, Ahmad sat where he was, gently holding the axe handle to relieve the pressure on his wound.

'You must not harm me,' a voice suddenly whispered. It was soft, gentle, as though leaves were rustling in the wind. 'You must not harm me,' the voice repeated. At first Ahmad thought he was hallucinating from the pain. But as he looked around for the culprit, he suddenly knew where the voice was coming from. The rain tree was talking to him. 'I am the spirit of your ancestors. You will get the land you need. Be patient, you are young. Be patient.'

The ambulance arrived and Ahmad was taken to A&E. The axe was removed and his wound was stitched up. Luckily it was not infected. A month later Ahmad's neighbours announced that they would sell some of their land to Ahmad if he promised not to cut down the tree. They liked the view they had of it from their garden. The price for the land was very fair, and the bank agreed.

Today Ahmad has a big farm and the most beautiful Golden Rain Tree in all of Singapore still stands where it has always stood.

Every day, as the sun is going down, Ahmad and his mother sit on the log bench under the tree, sipping tea. There they sit and listen to the rain tree's gentle whisper, its tears no longer raining down upon them.

# River girl

The converted shophouse was one of a dozen huddled near to the upper end of the Singapore River. Now the area has been swallowed up by bars, clubs and restaurants, but at the time of this story a small row of shophouses still remained.

It began with Owen Ng, whose family owned one of the shophouses. Over the decades they had rented it to various wealthy businessmen. Its ideal location and fantastic river views meant it had been prime real estate in Singapore for a long time. But even they had relented to the lure of making a huge profit by selling and had given in to a property developer who wanted to buy the shophouses en-bloc and replace them with new condos. Knowing that soon the shophouse would be demolished had prompted Owen to stay there one last time, even if it was just for a few weeks.

Having just returned from university in the UK, Owen had no apartment. He still hadn't made his mind up where he wanted to live, be it Singapore, Hong Kong or even Bangkok. With his double degree in Business Management and Accountancy, he was hot property as far as employers were concerned, but he was in no rush.

Having 'worked his butt off', as he put it, in London, he wanted to take some time out and enjoy himself before the real hard work began. So when his uncle, Harry, had suggested that he stay in the house for a few weeks before the developers moved in, he'd jumped at the chance. It had been fully converted into a residence years before so he would want for nothing. Because the deal was still going through, the actual date of demolition hadn't been set. It was agreed that Owen would stay there and take care of the property until a date was agreed. The other shophouses in the row had already been abandoned.

Not quite believing his luck, Owen and his English girlfriend, Caroline, who had also just graduated from university, moved into the shophouse. Although neither of them were working yet, Owen's father still gave him an allowance and Caroline had savings to tide her over until she got a job. The two quickly settled into a party lifestyle, eager to have some uncomplicated fun before their careers took over.

First on the list was a housewarming party. Owen invited all his friends from JC he hadn't seen in a couple of years, as well as university friends from London who had also returned to Singapore. Friends brought friends and soon there was a good mix of locals and expats alike.

The party was a blast. Owen, despite not being a drinker, still knew how to party. Caroline always boasted that he was great to go out with because at university he had been both a party animal and a sober driver to take her home at the end of the night. For Owen, he just wanted to make sure everyone had a good time.

It was the small hours of Sunday morning and the party was showing no signs of abating. Suddenly a girl began mingling amongst the revellers in the indoor courtyard. She must have been about eighteen or nineteen and looked like a mix of Chinese and Indian, a very striking combination. She was beautiful, tall, with long straight black hair. She was wearing a fitted black dress which not only looked very expensive but also a bit out of place amongst everyone else in shorts and T-shirts. The other unusual thing was that she wasn't wearing any shoes.

When Owen first noticed her she was smiling, surrounded by a group of guys who were each trying to impress her with drunken stories of acts of bravado. She was listening politely but saying very little. Owen caught her eye and waved. Then he moved on.

'She's hot and she's called Kim,' Andy Lim, Owen's oldest school friend, mumbled as he struggled to hold himself upright. Andy wasn't used to drinking and had already thrown up the contents of his stomach once that evening. It was clear he wouldn't be impressing anyone at this party.

Owen carried on mingling with his friends and when he next went to the courtyard area, Kim was gone. No one had seen her leave.

A while later Owen went upstairs to check on Caroline. She'd downed one drink too many and gone to lie down. The party was also starting to wind down. A group of people still hovered around, drinking and listening to music.

In the bedroom upstairs Caroline was out for the count, fully clothed but passed out on the bed. She'd covered her face with a damp face cloth. Owen closed the door quietly and was about to go downstairs when he heard a sound from the second bedroom. It made him stop. He was sure he'd locked that room to prevent anyone going in there and trashing the room. He was sure. But locked or not, there was definitely someone inside.

Owen tried the door. It *was* locked. Puzzled, he rummaged in the pocket of one of his jackets hanging from a hook in the corridor and found the key exactly where he'd left it. He opened the bedroom door. There, lying on the bed, was the girl in the expensive black dress. He could just make out that she was crying.

'How did you get in here?' he asked her.

'The door was open.'

'But I locked it.'

'I just walked in,' Kim replied. 'Can I stay in here, please?'

Owen hesitated for a moment. He really preferred she didn't but, well, she did seem upset about something. He relented.

'Okay. What's wrong? Anything I can do?'

'No one can help me. But thank you,' she replied.

'Will you be all right?'

Kim hesitated then smiled sadly.

'Yes, I will be all right.'

'Okay.' Owen started to close the door.

'Thank you,' she said.

'Yeah.' Owen pulled the door shut. He didn't lock it. Instead he put the key in the pocket of his shorts and went back down to the party to see how the casualties were coping.

As dawn broke the party ended. Several people crashed out in the shophouse while others staggered away looking for taxis to take them to their own beds. Owen picked his way through the bodies sprawled around the lounge and went upstairs. Caroline was still asleep. He quietly opened the door to the second bedroom to see two university friends sprawled out on the bed.

There was no sign of Kim. Owen shrugged and went to join Caroline.

Later that day, when everyone had gone home, Owen tidied up. Caroline was still hiding under the bedclothes. It was only when Owen was picking up empty beer cans from the internal courtyard that he found a pair of black high heels with a silver jewel on the front of each shoe. He thought someone would come and claim them, so he put them in a cupboard in the kitchen and forgot about them.

The next day Caroline went for an interview with a recruitment agency in the CBD. Owen decided to have breakfast at the local *kopitiam* and picked up a copy of *The Straits Times* on the way. He'd promised himself he would check out some of the job vacancies. Two weeks of doing nothing but partying was becoming quite boring—not to mention expensive. He and Caroline had agreed that they should start to focus on their careers.

Settling down to a cup of coffee and two slices of kaya toast, Owen took out the paper and froze. There, on the front page, was a photograph of Kim. He almost spat his coffee out in shock and began reading the article at breakneck speed. According to the report, the police had pulled a body from the Singapore River, near Boat Quay, the previous evening. The body had been identified as Kim Yap, a high-class escort. The police maintained that a concierge had been the last person to see her alive at about 1 am on Sunday morning, leaving one of Singapore's leading hotels. She'd wished him good night, as she usually did. Her image had been captured on the hotel's CCTV camera. The police had already spoken to the man who'd been her client that night. He'd reported that she had been in good spirits when she'd left and that their transaction had been pleasant with no drama.

The police pathologist had examined the body and estimated that she'd died in the early hours of Sunday morning. A small battery-powered alarm clock had also been found in her handbag and had stopped at 2.18 am. There had been no sign of physical abuse and the cause of death had been confirmed as drowning. Her handbag had washed up further down the river and everything she'd left the hotel with had been accounted for, even the $2,000 her client had paid her. The only missing item was the pair of shoes she'd been wearing that night—black high heels with a silver jewel on the front of each shoe.

Owen's brain went into overdrive. How could the girl have been at his party when she was already dead, drowned and floating in the Singapore River? How did her shoes get in his courtyard? How had she entered a locked bedroom?

Owen left the *kopitiam* and ran home. He fished the shoes out of the kitchen cupboard and stood with them dangling from his fingers. What the hell was he supposed to do with them? He knew that if he phoned the police and told them what had happened they'd never believe him, no matter how many witnesses there had been. As for her going through a locked door, well, he'd been the only witness to that. They'd throw him into a padded cell and throw away the key for good measure. With the shoes hidden in a paper bag, Owen headed down towards the river. Looking around to make sure that no one else was there, he removed the shoes from the bag and gently dropped them into the water. Afraid and confused, he watched them sink below the murky water.

# Occupied

My name is Laura Koh. I live in an apartment in Choa Chu Kang. I moved in four years ago. The previous occupants of the apartment had been an elderly couple. The husband had died first and the wife had stayed on in the apartment alone until she too passed away several years later.

I knew all of this before I moved in with my fourteen-year-old son, Chuan Wing. The thought that people had died in the apartment never bothered me. I am a hospice nurse and I nursed my husband through cancer until he died.

I think nurses, particularly those who care for terminally ill patients, appreciate the gift of life and how precious it is. I suppose I do what I do because I want to give people as good an end to their life as possible.

So Chuan Wing and I moved into Block 683, #08–08 one Saturday in 2004. It was a small apartment with two bedrooms but that, of course, was enough for us. From the apartment we could see Kranji Reservoir and the sea beyond.

Because Chuan Wing had a desktop computer and desk, I gave him the larger of the two bedrooms. It was important for him to be able to do his schoolwork in peace and quiet. I didn't mind having the smaller bedroom because it also had a lovely view.

The first night we camped in the apartment surrounded by boxes and suitcases. We ate at the hawker centre downstairs and slept in the lounge on mattresses.

The next day was Sunday, and Chuan Wing and I, along with my brother, Addy, and his wife, Felicia, assembled our beds and other furniture and put everything in its place. Felicia brought us all chicken rice for lunch and when they had gone, Chuan Wing and I stood and looked around our new home.

'I like it, Ma,' Chuan Wing said, giving me a big hug. I had to agree with him and when he went to his bedroom to work, I went to my room and began unpacking my clothes, hanging them in the wardrobe and arranging things in my bedside cabinet. The bed took up most of the room but I didn't mind. I would only be using the bedroom to sleep in. Now I had a new kitchen and a big living room with a view. I was possibly happier at that moment than at any other time since my husband's illness.

When I had finished unpacking my clothes, I put the empty suitcases at the back of the wardrobe. Felicia had helped me make the bed. Satisfied that everything was neat and tidy, I went into the kitchen to make noodle soup. Our first dinner in our new home would be a simple one.

After we had eaten, I decided to have an early night. I had to work the next day and still hadn't decided how I was going to get there. I knew I would have to allow extra time to get from our new flat in Choa Chu Kang to the hospice where I worked. I would have to take the MRT then a bus because I didn't have a car. Whether it would be faster to take the bus all the way I would discover in the days ahead.

After I had a shower I said good night to Chuan Wing and warned him not to work too late. I went to bed and fell asleep very quickly, exhausted and happy to be in our nice new home. I always like to be woken up by the sun and that night, with no tall buildings between my room and my precious view, I kept the curtains open.

I don't know what time it happened but it was long before dawn. I woke in my bed to feel someone or something tilting the mattress. I suddenly realised I had rolled against the wall and that was what had woken me. The edge of the mattress was in the air above me. Someone had lifted it up, causing me to roll over.

'Chuan Wing!' I scolded. 'What are you doing?' There was no reply and that was when I wondered if it was indeed my son. I scrambled to the end of the bed and stepped onto the floor. As I did so, the side of the mattress fell back down onto the bed. There was enough light from the window for me to see there was no one there at all.

Needless to say I was shaken, if not a little scared. I went and checked on Chuan Wing. Like most growing boys, he slept deeply. He hadn't stirred from the commotion in my bedroom. I closed his door quietly and went to get a glass of juice. I sat with my drink and wondered what had just happened. I was still sitting there when the sun rose.

The next day at work I mentioned what had happened to one of my colleagues. Suhana is Malay and very superstitious, so it is perhaps a little strange that she is a hospice nurse as she deals with death regularly. However, she has been doing the job for years and seems to have a good balance in life. Suhana told me she had heard of similar experiences, and that she would speak to her auntie in Melaka and ask her advice. Apparently this auntie was something of an expert in this sort of thing.

In the meantime life carried on as normal. The next few nights nothing happened to my bed, but it must have been around the fourth night when I awoke to the same thing. The side of the mattress was high in the air, as though someone was violently shaking it.

'Stop it!' I shouted as I scrambled to the end of the bed. Once again the mattress hung in the air for a moment before falling back down to the bed frame. After the first time it had happened, I'd tried to lift the mattress myself but hadn't been able to, and I was used to lifting people in and out of bed at work. Whoever or whatever was lifting it in the air was very, very strong.

I told Suhana about my latest experience and she immediately apologised—she had forgotten to call her auntie and promised to do it that night just as soon as she got home.

That night things were different. I left my bedroom neat and tidy and went and had a shower. Chuan Wing was in his room. I hadn't told him about my bed and what had been happening. He had slept through it both times and I didn't want to alarm him unduly. Whatever was happening was focussed on me and my bed, or so it seemed.

When I went back to my room after my shower, I couldn't believe my eyes. The mattress, bedding still attached, was leaning against the wall. The pillows were scattered on the floor.

'That's enough,' I said firmly. 'That is definitely enough!' I was angry. I didn't know whatever entity was messing up my bed. I didn't know if I believed in spirits but right then I didn't care. I was so angry! I pulled the mattress down again, straightened the bedclothes and put the pillows back on the bed. 'Go away!' I snapped. 'I have had enough of you.'

With that I climbed into bed. I didn't switch off the light but instead sat and pretended to read a book. Nothing happened and eventually I switched the light off and went to sleep. I expected the spirit, or whatever it was, to come back again that night. It didn't.

'Female spirit,' Suhana said as soon as I met her the next morning.

'It's her house and she doesn't want another woman living in it. She's jealous and she wants you to leave. You're sleeping in her bedroom.'

'All of that from one phone call?' I replied.

'My auntie says it could be like a *mumiai*, a Malay poltergeist that throws things around inside the house. It's the most common spirit problem of all.'

'So how do I deal with it?'

'Talisman,' Suhana replied. 'My auntie is sending it to me today. You say some words in every room, burn incense then put the talisman above your door. The spirit leaves your house and when the talisman is put in place, it can't come back inside. Simple.' She was so matter-of-fact about it all that I felt reassured.

That night the mattress was again standing against the wall when I came back from the bathroom. Pillows were on the floor and the drawers of my bedside cabinet had been opened, their contents strewn around the room. It seemed that the spirit of the old lady who had lived and died in the apartment was getting angrier with me by the day.

I tidied everything up and eventually got into bed. I fell sleep but after a short while I was violently woken again. Something was shaking my mattress and I was once again jammed up against the wall.

'Old woman, go away!' I shouted. This time Chuan Wing

woke up. My bedroom door opened just as I was scrambling off the end of the bed. He switched on the light and saw the edge of the mattress in the air just before it fell back down to the bed frame.

'Ma?' he asked, startled more than frightened, I think. 'What's going on?'

'I'll explain later,' I told him as I found a dressing gown. I needed a hot drink. I don't drink alcohol but if I'd had a drop in the house then I would have drunk it.

I told Chuan Wing what had been happening and he got quite angry at the fact that I hadn't told him before. At that moment I couldn't help feeling proud of him. As the man of the household he was starting to take responsibility, and protecting his mother was a job he took seriously.

The package from Suhana's auntie arrived the next morning. Suhana said that she would come home with me after work and we would do the spell together. I was thankful for that.

On the MRT ride to my apartment she told me that she had done this kind of thing many times. Some of the people she personally nursed were very superstitious. Malays would ask for her at the hospital because of her background and understanding of things spiritual.

'They ask me to say a spell to help them pass over and to help their families when they're gone,' she explained. 'I like to help them any way I can.' I looked at Suhana. Even though I'd known her for many years, I'd never seen this side to her.

When we got to the apartment, Chuan Wing was still at school, which made it easier. From her handbag Suhana took the talisman, which was in a small cloth bag the size of a matchbox. She carefully put it to one side of the front door.

'If we put it in place now, the spirit of the old lady won't be able to get out,' she explained. 'Most spirits have to be invited to enter a house through the door and leave the same way. Not all spirits, but most, and in this case because she is the former owner, through the front door is the only way she can leave or enter. We will tell her to leave, and when she's gone we'll put the talisman in place so she can never enter again. She will then have to travel to wherever her spirit can find peace.'

Suhana and I entered the apartment. She handed me some incense sticks and instructed me to make sure that the smoke got into every corner of the apartment as she was casting her spell. We left the apartment door wide open and started going from room to room, she chanting her spells, me waving the incense. We started in the back rooms and finally moved to the living room, walking backwards and forwards across it until we arrived at the front door.

Suhana walked outside and I followed. She picked up the talisman and placed it on the ledge above the door. Then she nailed it in place. Because I didn't have a hammer we had to use my meat cleaver, but it worked. The talisman was fixed permanently above the door.

And that was the end of the ghost of the old woman. We never heard from her again. Chuan Wing and I still live in the apartment and I imagine I will be there until I die. After I'm dead, will my spirit haunt the bedroom and try and drive away the new woman of the house? I certainly hope not.

# From beyond the grave

They gathered around the grave. It was the rainy season and rain it did. Only a handful of mourners were there to pay their last respects, including the priest, the undertaker and his assistant. It was a meagre turnout.

The old man had not been popular but he'd also managed to outlive the few friends he had had. Those at the funeral were mainly family and extended family. The reading of the will was scheduled to take place later that day, and several of the mourners had travelled from as far afield as the United Kingdom and Australia to be there. But they weren't there to grieve—they were there to fight over the financial remains of one of Singapore's wealthiest men.

Roger Young had been a rich man, a very rich man indeed. Banking, investments, property and a few under-the-table deals had propelled him into high society. It was even rumoured that he had links with some very unscrupulous people and that some of his fortune had come from criminal activities.

'He was buried with a mobile phone,' one of the mourners whispered to another.

'I heard that,' came the reply. 'Bit stupid really, especially if there was an autopsy and he was embalmed.'

'He wasn't,' whispered Amelia Stanton, a niece of the dead man. 'No need for an autopsy because his personal doctor confirmed he'd died from a heart condition.'

'He had a heart?' replied James, her cousin.

'Yes, he was a mean old sod,' Amelia agreed.

'And what about being embalmed?' James asked.

'No, he stipulated no embalming. He's been buried intact.'

'Ninety years old and a resurrection complex,' James snorted. They both smiled.

'Bloody rain,' Amelia said, brushing a hand across her face. James tilted his umbrella to shield his cousin from the downpour. She'd been to too many funerals in her short lifetime. Five years before, Amelia had buried her husband, Stephen, the victim of a bike accident in Malaysia. Since then she'd been raising her two sons alone. She'd never remarried, despite being only thirty-nine. During her hardship as a single mother, Roger Young had never once offered a penny of support.

By contrast her cousin James was a player. Married twice, divorced once and heading towards his second divorce, he was looking around for wife number three, both in his native Australia and further afield. Singapore was somewhere he hadn't yet tried. He was tall with thick fair hair. Like Amelia he was part-Chinese. His mother Patricia, Roger's sister, had married a blonde Englishman who'd handed down his fair hair to his son. Both

Patricia and Roger were the children of James Young, an English army officer, and Helen Wong, a teacher from Hong Kong. They'd settled in Singapore when the children were young.

The priest was intoning fine words about the man who most of those standing around the grave despised intensely. Roger had not had any family. Some said the reason for his childless state was the fact that he was too mean to part with any of his money. Judith, his English wife of many tortured years, had passed away at the age of seventy and Roger, some ten years older, had never deigned to remarry.

When the priest finished, various speakers reluctantly stepped up to say a few words. First was the dead man's lawyer. He said a few neutral but carefully chosen words, then quietly left the cemetery for another appointment, this time with the living. James had no intention whatsoever of speaking, and it appeared that many of the other distant and not-so-distant relatives shared his view.

The Lord's Prayer was the penultimate act, followed by the recitation of 'dust to dust, ashes to ashes', which brought a smile to Amelia's face.

'Mud to mud,' she whispered to her cousin. James chuckled.

'Well if the old bugger comes back to life, now is definitely the time to use his mobile phone,' James quipped as the ornate casket began to descend into the ground, each mourner contemplating the fact that one day it would be his turn. No matter how much money you had, death was inevitable.

Two labourers, huddled under a large umbrella several metres behind the minister, waited patiently for the mourners to leave. It was their job to fill in the grave, despite the rain.

'I need a stiff drink,' James whispered to his cousin.

'Me too,' she replied. 'My maid is looking after the boys. Why don't we go to the Long Bar at Raffles and order a couple of gin and tonics? It's after noon so it should be open.'

Since her husband's death Amelia didn't go out much. He hadn't left them well-off and, with two demanding children and an equally demanding job, her social life was almost non-existent. Her cousin was great fun, and Amelia hoped he would at least join her for a drink.

'Of course,' James said, taking Amelia's arm and leading the charge to the waiting cars.

The reading of the will was scheduled for 4.30 pm in the offices of Talbot & Strange on Victoria Street. It was only 1.30 pm. They had plenty of time to kill.

As the mourners departed, the two labourers set about removing the grass matting from around the grave and shovelling dirt on top of the coffin.

The thudding sound awoke him.

He lay in the darkness and tried to orientate himself.

'Buried,' Roger Young blurted. His voice was a muted croak, his throat, his mouth, his lips all as dry as sandpaper. 'Alive,' he added. His greatest fear of being buried alive had been realised. 'Alive,' he repeated. 'I'm alive.'

The sound of the clods of earth landing on the casket was loud. The old man called out, but his voice was feeble. He tried again but above the grave, their heads covered by rain jackets, the two labourers couldn't hear a thing.

The phone, he remembered. Although the confines of the casket pressed in on him, he had just enough freedom to move his arms. He found the phone where he had insisted it be left—in his left jacket pocket. After a few attempts he managed to get it where he could see it and flipped it open. The blue light was comforting, as were the numbers and the SMS he had programmed into it.

There were three numbers that would receive the SMS simultaneously. One was his lawyer, Michael Talbot. Another was the widow Amelia. And finally there was Edric, his assistant of twenty-five years.

Roger managed to retrieve the SMS and pressed 'send'. Before the signal could die completely and more earth cover the tomb, the pre-set text message was sent.

It simply read:

*I have been buried alive.*

*Rescue me.*

*Roger Young*

He was sure that soon they would alert the undertakers. In the meantime the old man would wait. Due to his pathological fear of being buried alive, the tycoon had insisted that there be a cylinder of oxygen placed inside his casket, as well as the mobile phone. The air in the coffin was thick and foul. The cylinder lay at his right side. Using his right hand, he turned on the valve. There was enough oxygen to keep him alive for several hours, if he was frugal with it. He knew that in perhaps as little as half an hour he would be free.

Amelia's handbag hung from the bar stool. The stress of the morning, and indeed of the past few months, finally surfaced and she was already on her second gin and tonic.

'Steady on,' James warned, 'we've got all afternoon.'

'Sorry, it's just that . . . well . . . things have been hard since Stephen died. Sometimes I don't know how I will cope.' Feeling slightly embarrassed, James shifted in his seat. He didn't really know what to say. Comforting widows wasn't really his forte. 'Sorry,' Amelia repeated. 'Excuse me, I'm just going to the ladies.' She hopped off the bar stool and headed back through the bar.

Neither of them heard the faint whirr of the mobile phone coming from her handbag.

Michael Talbot, Roger's lawyer, was in a meeting. He was a stickler for making sure all mobile phones were switched off when he was with clients. There was no exception to the rule.

Edric Lee, Roger's assistant, was sitting in the back of the taxi on his way to Changi Airport. He was flying to Hong Kong to be with his family and would not be returning to Singapore.

For twenty-five years he had been in Singapore employed by Roger Young. Those twenty-five years had not been good years; his employer had been a harsh mean man. Edric would have left years ago but for Roger's wife, Judith. The pair of them had discovered a love of sorts, driven together by her tyrannical domineering husband.

While Roger had dedicated himself to increasing his fortune by whatever means possible, Judith and Edric had become close friends. Roger's long business trips gave them time to grow closer and, over time, they had fallen in love. Edric had even contemplated killing the monster at one point and running away with the lovely Mrs Young. When she'd died, his whole world collapsed. But he hadn't left. He'd stayed for one reason and one reason only.

Edric looked across at his bag on the seat next to him. Inside it was a large sum of money and several extremely valuable pieces of jade—all gifts from the late Mrs Young, all legally certified. She had left them to him in her will and without the knowledge of her husband. Edric had always feared that somehow Roger would have stopped him from having them if he'd known. So he'd waited and waited. And now, with the old man dead, he was free to collect what was rightfully his. He was about to start a new life as a very wealthy man.

The mobile phone in Edric's pocket chimed. He removed it and flipped it open. There was an SMS. He read the message several times, smiled and pressed the delete button.

'Shall we go?' It was only twenty minutes before the will was to be read and James didn't want to be late.

'Sure. Hold on a second, I just need to call home and see if the boys are okay.' Amelia reached into her handbag and retrieved her phone. James watched as she flipped it open but instead of dialling a number, she seemed to be reading something. Suddenly she thrust the phone at him. He read the text message and grimaced.

'The old man didn't even have the decency to say please,' was all he said as he handed the phone back to Amelia.

'What do we do?'

'Did he ever do anything for you?'

'No. Never,' Amelia admitted.

'We went to his funeral today. Let's leave it at that,' James replied.

'I guess.' Amelia opened the phone again, pressed delete and put it back into her handbag.

Michael Talbot finished his meeting. He went to the bathroom then asked for a cup of coffee to be brought into his office. The family of the recently departed Roger Young would soon be arriving for the reading of the will. This was something that the lawyer wasn't looking forward to. The old man had left his family nothing. All his fortune was going to an anonymous charity. The lawyer had tried to dissuade the tycoon from committing such a foul deed, but his client had been adamant. This was going to be his final snub from beyond the grave to what he called 'those circling vultures'.

Michael suggested that Roger should at least leave something to his assistant Edric as a small token of appreciation for his years of loyalty but his client had dismissed the suggestion, laughing at such a ridiculous idea.

'That man has been stealing from me for years,' he said. 'He has been robbing me blind. I have no doubt about it so, no, he gets nothing, no one gets anything.'

'But a charity you don't have any connection to?'

'All the better,' the old man had chortled, 'all the better!'

The oxygen was running out and still no one had come to release him. Roger called out but his voice echoed around the coffin, thin and lost. It was getting hot now. He had tried using the phone to call someone but there was no signal now that six feet of soil had been packed on top of him.

'Please come for me,' he whimpered. 'Please come for me.'

Now he was starting to panic, his heart pounding violently in his chest.

'Please come for me!'

As the family members filed into the lawyer's office, Michael Talbot checked his mobile phone. He had forgotten to switch it back on since his other meeting. There were several voice messages and one SMS. When he read the message, the startled lawyer grimaced. Then he read it again and smiled. He pressed the delete button and switched off his phone.

'Goodbye forever, you mean old tyrant!'

'Please, somebody, please . . . somebody . . . please . . .' Roger Young's final pleas faded into nothingness. Up above, the rain stopped and the sun broke through the grey November sky.

# The Bogeyman

'They say he only comes out on nights when the moon is full. Nights like tonight!' Madam Tay masked a smile from the dozen girls seated in a semi-circle around her. 'Nights just like tonight,' she repeated.

A collective shiver ran through the girls, not just from the storyteller's words but from a draught in the room. Beside the teacher was a large fat candle nestled in a tall iron candelabra. It was the room's only source of light. It flickered and almost died.

The class sleepover was an annual event for Madam Tay's class of ten-year-old girls. It was highly anticipated, both by the parents, the girls themselves and, if truth be told, by Madam Tay herself. Story night was always an exciting break from the monotony of the school year. The ritual was always the same. Parents would drop their children back at the school at 6.30 pm on the night of a full moon during the last term of the school year. Each girl would come equipped with snacks, a pillow, a toothbrush, a pair of pyjamas and a change of clothes for the next day.

'Yes,' Madam Tay continued dramatically, 'nights just like this are when The Bogeyman comes.' Squeals of anticipation and mock terror filled the room. The candle flickered again as if on cue and startled even Madam Tay. She couldn't imagine where the draught could be coming from. It was a typically warm humid night and she'd switched off the air-con before the girls had arrived.

She continued. 'He's tall and his skin is green, like old leather left in the rain.' Sensing the growing tension, the girls held hands, their eyes wide as they hung onto their teacher's every word. 'His hair is like rotting seaweed, hanging down his back, almost touching the ground.' Her voice became more animated. 'His eyes blaze like the fires of a furnace and his teeth, what wicked teeth they are, sharper than knives.' Madam Tay had always been a fine storyteller. She'd studied drama at university and was adept at using her voice and facial expressions to create scenarios that terrified her audience. Some of the girls had covered their ears with their hands but this was just all part of the act. Really they didn't want to miss a single word of this scary story.

'Teeth like those of a shark. They are razor sharp and as yellow as a smoker's smile.' Every year Madam Tay took this opportunity to reinforce the anti-smoking message she and the school promoted heavily. 'Yes,' she added, 'the yellow of a smoker's smile. The breath of The Bogeyman stinks like sulphur and rotting meat. It hovers about him like a green gas.'

The candle flickered again but this time it was nearly extinguished. The draught had become stronger, but rather than investigate and break the flow of her tale, Madam Tay decided to keep going. She slipped one hand behind her back, her fingers touching the cold metal of a torch. Reassured, she picked up the pace of her tale.

'When The Bogeyman walks, you can hear the squelch of blood in his boots because when he captures a victim, he tears their throat out with his wicked yellow teeth.' She paused again for effect. 'When he tears the throat out of the unfortunate boy or girl he has caught, he holds the body above his head and opens his mouth to drink their blood.' Madam Tay held her arms above her head and opened her mouth, imitating the drinking demon. She eventually lowered her arms and her voice was filled with an unholy relish. 'The blood he doesn't catch in his mouth runs down his chest and down his legs into his boots.'

The girls squealed and most of them hid their faces against the shoulders of their neighbours. Madam Tay smiled as she continued, her voice filling the room.

'Then, carrying the body of his victim over his shoulder, The Bogeyman returns to the dark place from where he has come.' She began speaking slower and lowered her voice for dramatic effect. 'There, sitting in his throne by hell's fire, The Bogeyman's demon servants take off his long boots. They hold them aloft, turn them upside down and pour the leftover blood into a large crystal goblet. And when that is done The Bogeyman sits, drinking the blood as he watches the body of his unfortunate victim roasting on the spit before him.'

Madam Tay looked around the room. She was pleased with the reaction she was getting. Every year she would make up stories on the spur of the moment, carried along by the frenzy and fear of the night of the full moon. This one was turning out to be one of her finest efforts. The girls were transfixed, their little imaginations running wild, much to their teacher's delight. Their little bodies were all bunched together as, terrified, they clung to each other's arms. Instead of hiding their faces in mock horror, they stared ahead, their pale faces shining in the flickering candlelight, their eyes bulging.

Imagination, Madam Tay thought, smiling quietly to herself. She always tried to encourage her students to use their imaginations and this was one way of doing just that. In her opinion a little horror tale or two allowed their imaginations to break free of convention and create worlds they could only dream of. She continued, pleased with how well the sleepover was going.

'And when the last of the blood is drunk, and the body on the spit is done, The Bogeyman makes his demon servants bring him the iron spit. They stand in front of him, their hands burning from the heat of the iron rods. As they scream in pain their master begins to tear hunks of roasted meat from the roasted body, devouring them piece by piece.'

The girls screamed wildly but this time Madam Tay could detect a real fear in their voices. Startled, she looked around the room and saw that some were pointing towards her while others were hiding their faces in their hands. Never before had she experienced a reaction quite as dramatic as this.

'Teacher, The Bogeyman,' one girl shouted.

'Behind you, Teacher,' another yelled as the screaming grew louder, more frantic, more terrified, more genuine. For a split second Madam Tay wondered if the girls had decided to turn the tables on her, ganging up to terrify *her* instead of the other way around. She chuckled, just as she smelt the strong odour of sulphur and a rising cold draught tickle the back of her neck. The fat candle next to her flickered and died.

Terrified, Madam Tay turned her head and there, standing behind her, glowing green, with eyes like fire and teeth that gleamed yellow, stood The Bogeyman.

He lunged towards her.